The Time Witches

The Time Witches

MICHAEL MOLLOY

SCHOLASTIC INC.

New York Toronto London Auckland Sydney
Mexico City New Delhi Hong Kong Buenos Aires

ISBN 0-439-42090-3

12 11 10 9 8 7 6 5 4 3 2   2 3 4 5 6 7/0
                                                        40

Cover design by Elizabeth Parisi and Steve Scott.
Text design by Dorchester Typesetting Group Ltd.

Printed in the U.S.A.
First Scholastic printing, September 2002

For Jane,
Kate, and Alex

Contents

The Time Witches

1

The Secret of Lucia Cheeseman's Cottage

It was a warm summer's day in Speller, the little seaside town where Abby Clover lived. But in Darkwood Forest, the great woodland that lay beyond the cliffs, a cold rain was falling.

The heavy downpour drenched a shabby figure trudging wearily through the thick underbrush beneath the ancient canopy of weeping trees. The man, carrying a large suitcase, was trying to keep up with a raven. It flitted from branch to branch, deeper and deeper into the tangled wood. Suddenly, the man stumbled on a tree root and stopped.

"Just wait a minute, you blasted bird," he hissed when he had caught his breath, "I want to take a break."

The raven folded its wings and sat in the hollow of a dead oak tree, watching the man with unblinking eyes as he adjusted his black hat to stop the rainwater from trickling inside the collar of his crumpled coat.

"Is it much farther?" the man asked impatiently.

The raven gave a croak of contempt and flew deeper into the forest. Cursing, the shabby figure picked up his suitcase and followed, his shoes squelching through the mud.

As he proceeded, he was aware of slight rustlings all about

him. He felt unseen eyes watching his progress but, no matter how hard he looked, he saw only the dripping greenery of the forest.

Eventually, the bird led the man into a dismal clearing where a lichen-covered cottage, built of crumbling yellow bricks, stood beneath an overhang of dead trees. Foul-smelling smoke curled lazily from the crooked chimney, and poison ivy grew around the flaking door. With a final croak, the raven made for an opening beneath the eaves of the cottage and hopped inside.

The man stood before the door and kicked it. "Mother," he called impatiently. "Open up, it's me, Wolfbane."

"Just a minute," a rather haughty voice answered. "I'm doing something."

"Get a move on," Wolfbane replied. "I'm soaked through."

After a minute, there was the sound of a bolt being drawn and the door creaked open. Wolfbane felt a wave of nostalgia as a powerful odor of mold and decay filled his nostrils.

"All your homes smell the same, Mother. It takes me back to my childhood," he said. He stepped over the threshold and looked about the gloomy interior as his mother returned to what she was doing.

The single room was crammed with dusty glass bottles. Some were filled with strange liquids, powders, crystals, and dried herbs. Others held dead lizards, bats, snakes, and a variety of insects. The bottles covered most of the stone floor and the shelves that lined the room.

In the fireplace, a black iron cauldron containing a thick bubbling concoction hung over a smoldering fire.

Propped open on a greasy wooden table by the window was a hefty, leather-bound book. Wolfbane's mother stood, gazing down at the pages with a slight frown on her face. She looked up and glanced in disapproval at her son's disheveled appearance.

As always, Lucia Cheeseman was dressed in the latest Paris fashion. Her hair was immaculate and her makeup flawless. Despite the squalor of her surroundings, she looked as if she were about to attend a royal garden party.

"You look quite dreadful, darling," she said accusingly.

Wolfbane shrugged. "So would you if you'd been following that blasted raven of yours through a soaking wet forest. Why didn't you lay a poison path? I think there are elves about."

"There *are* elves about, but other people can follow a poison path," she replied sharply. "I like my privacy. That's why I arranged for Caspar to guide you."

"Well, I swear he brought me the long way around," grumbled Wolfbane. "We kept passing the same dead tree."

Caspar, now perched on a rafter above them, gave a soft croak and rested his head on his chest in a satisfied fashion.

"It's your own fault," Lucia said briskly. "You used to torment him when you were a child."

"He never liked me," Wolfbane replied sulkily. "That's why I used to pull out his feathers."

"Don't whine, darling," Lucia continued. "Your father and I didn't send you to the best boarding schools to become a whiner. Now, why did you contact me? What do you want?"

"I need to hide out for a while," Wolfbane replied as he hung his dripping coat and hat near the fire and carefully placed his suitcase in a corner of the room.

"And where did you get that dreadful face?" his mother asked as Wolfbane leaned forward to kiss her on the dead-white cheek she offered.

"Don't you like it?" he said, turning to examine his fat, jovial features in the grimy fly-specked mirror over the fireplace.

"You look like a village butcher," she answered.

Wolfbane nodded. "That's a pretty good guess. I took it from a Mr. Button in Wiltshire. He *was* the local butcher."

"What were you doing in Wiltshire?" she asked, her gaze returning to the leather-bound book.

"Hiding from the Light Witches. They've been hunting me, you know."

Lucia nodded. "I read all about it in *The Witch Times*."

Wolfbane looked aghast. "How did they get hold of the story? What did they say?"

"See for yourself," she answered, gesturing toward a bowl of water on the table next to the book. "They did a long interview with that dreadful man Chadwick Street."

Wolfbane threw a coin into the dish and, as the ripples cleared, a headline formed. LIGHT WITCHES WIN THE BATTLE FOR ICE DUST. THE WITCH TRADE RESUMED. FULL REPORT ON PAGE SEVEN.

Wolfbane passed his hand over the surface and a page of words and pictures appeared. At the top was a large photograph of Abby Clover, Spike, Hilda Bluebell, Sir Chadwick Street, Captain Starlight, and the Great Mandini.

Lucia Cheeseman stood at her son's shoulder and also studied the picture. "So they're the ones who got the better of you," she said sharply. "Who is who?"

Wolfbane stiffened at her words and pointed to one of the figures in the photograph. It was a tall, handsome man with a Roman nose. Longish red hair and side-whiskers flowed from beneath his battered broad-brimmed hat. He wore a well-tailored three-piece tweed suit with a flowing red polka-dot bow tie. "You know *Sir* Chadwick Street, of course," Wolfbane said, adding a sarcastic emphasis to the title.

"Yes, yes," Lucia said impatiently. "I knew him even before he was Master of the Light Witches. Your father and I saw him on the stage before he received his knighthood. We always thought he was a terrible actor."

Wolfbane raised his eyebrows. "I didn't know you and Father were theatergoers."

Lucia waved her hand airily. "We never missed a production of *Macbeth*. Your father was fond of the three witches that come on at the beginning." She looked at the photograph again. "And who are the others?"

Wolfbane pointed at a smiling girl with a long face and hair the color of chestnuts, worn in pigtails. She had a snub nose dusted with freckles and dark green eyes. "That's Abby Clover," he hissed. "How I detest that meddlesome child." Then his finger went to a serious-looking boy with light blue eyes and the palest hair and skin Lucia had ever seen.

"They call this one Spike," he continued. "But he's actually Altur, Prince of Lantua and Lord of the Cold Seas."

Lucia nodded. "He's the one who can talk to sea creatures and swim like a fish."

"Yes," said Wolfbane. "The fair-haired woman with the silly dreamy expression is Hilda Bluebell. She's Chadwick Street's assistant, but I think they're romantically linked as well."

"Go on," said Lucia.

Wolfbane pointed again. "That one is Captain Adam Starlight."

"Hmmm," said Lucia, leaning forward to examine the picture more closely. The figure Wolfbane indicated was dressed in a sailor's pea jacket and a captain's hat. His trousers were tucked into high sea boots. He was tall and spare, and his bearded face was as brown as old leather. A long white scar ran down his jawbone.

"The Ancient Mariner," Lucia said softly. "He's the one who personally destroyed so many of your Shark Boats — and he's not even a Light Witch."

"But he's got an albatross called Benbow," Wolfbane explained. "And you know how powerful bewitched creatures can be."

Lucia pointed to an extraordinarily slim man in the photograph. He wore a white tie and tails and he had sharp, clever eyes and a pencil-thin mustache. His shiny black hair was so flat that it appeared to be painted onto his head. "So this must be the Great Mandini," she said. "For some reason I thought he would be fat."

"Sometimes he is," sniffed Wolfbane. "The blasted man can make himself any shape he wants. He's a magician."

Wolfbane began to read the story accompanying the picture. After studying the page, he snarled. "Usual trash journalism! Chadwick Street didn't capture *all* my stock of Black Dust. The suitcase I brought with me is full of it."

"Oh, good," Lucia exclaimed. "I've been wanting to try some of that."

"You can only have a few pinches," Wolfbane told her. "I'll need the rest."

"What for?"

"Somehow, I'm going to have my vengeance on Sir Chadwick Street and that child Abby Clover."

With that, he reached up and clawed the fat, smiling mask from his face and threw the quivering handful of rubbery material into the fire.

Lucia now smiled on the true features of her son. A sharp, cruel face that looked as if it had been carved from dead white stone gazed back at her. Only the slanting yellow eyes gave it color and life.

"By the way," he said, "how many elves are there in this forest? I felt there were eyes watching me all the time I was following the raven."

"Hundreds," Lucia answered, and she made a circle over her heart to ward off the elf curse before turning back to her book.

"Elves!" Wolfbane repeated with a shudder. "I can't stand the little vermin."

"They tickled your Uncle Ronnie to death, you know," said Lucia.

Wolfbane looked through the rain-streaked window into

the little clearing. "You've told me often enough. How is it there are so many here?"

Before she answered, Lucia took a pinch of yellow herbs from a jar and sprinkled it into the cauldron bubbling over the fire. "They were brought here ages ago by a man called Jack Elvin," she said. "The story is that he found them somewhere in the north. I believe Jack Elvin eventually settled in Speller."

As Wolfbane continued to glare out of the window, a thought began to stir in his mind. "There's something familiar about that name, *Elvin* . . ." he said slowly. Then he looked at Lucia. "Do you know how I can break into the *Light Witch Chronicles* they keep in their London library, Mother?"

"Of course I do," Lucia replied. She waved her hand over the bowl of water and chanted:

"Steal and sneak the work of others,
Thieves and robbers be our brothers,
Let this water show the past
That all Light Witches hold so fast."

"There," Lucia said with a wave. "Just speak the name and the reference will appear. But don't take too long. They have a security spell on the library. It will take effect after a few minutes."

"Jack Elvin," Wolfbane said, and words began to materialize in the bowl of water. He read quickly.

"Ah!" he said triumphantly. "Just as I thought. Jack Elvin was the ancestor of that dreadful child Abby Clover."

As the words faded, Lucia cleared the table and set out two large, greasy bowls. "Have some lunch. I've been cooking it all morning."

Wolfbane sat down and seized a spoon. After trying a few mouthfuls, he asked, "What's in this?"

Lucia shrugged. "Just a few things Caspar collected for me in the fields and woods. I call it carrion stew."

"It's delicious," Wolfbane said, greedily filling his bowl to the top again. "I suppose that bird does have his uses."

Lucia smiled up at the raven. "I don't know where I'd be without him." Looking back at her son, she said, "You should get yourself a familiar, dear. Every Night Witch should have one."

Wolfbane picked up a stewed creature on his spoon. "These rodents really are delicious. I've never seen a finer rat."

"That's not a rat, it's a mouse," Lucia replied.

"A mouse! This size — surely not?"

Lucia smiled in triumph. "I've perfected a new concoction. I call it Bigger Powder. Clever, aren't I?"

"Exceedingly so, Mother. Although the name seems a little obvious."

"Tush," said Lucia. "You always were too smart for your own good. A proper Night Witch always keeps things simple."

When Wolfbane had finished his meal, he sat back with a large glass of deadly nightshade brandy. Then he traced the name Abby Clover into the grease on the table. "That accursed child," he muttered. "I'll have my vengeance on Chadwick Street and Abby Clover."

"Why don't you just head over to Speller? It's only a few miles away. I happen to know Chadwick Street is there at the moment. You could dispose of them both today," said Lucia lightly.

Wolfbane shook his head. "Speller is full of Ice Dust. Even the whitewash on the walls of the cottages is mixed with it.

That's why we never raided Speller. It would have killed us. You know we Night Witches can't live around too much Ice Dust."

"I was only teasing," said Lucia. "Can't you protect yourself with Black Dust?"

Wolfbane shook his head. "All I have left is one rotten suitcase full. I need to get my enemies to a place where they only have access to a small amount of Ice Dust. Then we would have a fair contest."

Lucia nodded. She knew that, not long ago, Wolfbane had almost destroyed the Light Witches. Despite the danger to himself, he had discovered a way of mixing pure Ice Dust, the special ingredient in all Light Witch spells, with Dirt Dust, the powder Night Witches used in their magic. The result was Black Dust, the most powerful weapon for evil the world had ever seen.

He had been poised to destroy all the Light Witches, but Abby Clover and her friends had fought back and finally beaten the Night Witches in a great battle. Wolfbane had only just managed to escape.

Now Lucia smiled at him and said, "There's always the past, you know. The Wizards only allow Light Witches to travel back in time with a limited amount of Ice Dust. One wandful, I believe."

Wolfbane nodded. "If there were any justice, I could go back and wipe out her entire family before they got started."

"Then why don't you?" Lucia asked, raising her glass of brandy to her lips.

Wolfbane sighed. "You know as well as I do, Mother, that the Wizards have controlled time travel ever since they made us sign the Treaty with the Light Witches. I can't see them giving me a permit when I say I want to pop back to the past and exterminate a family that has been giving me trouble."

Lucia wiped out the bowls with a greasy cloth and put them in a cupboard under the stairs before she spoke. Straightening up, she patted her hair and said, "There's more than one way to time travel. The Wizards haven't always controlled it."

Wolfbane sighed again. "I know, but it's been such a long time that everyone has forgotten how it was done. The records were destroyed under the terms of the treaty. It's a lost art."

When Wolfbane saw Lucia was smirking, his heart gave a little leap. "You know something, Mother," he said excitedly. "What is it?"

Chuckling, Lucia said, "Why do you think I came back to this wretched place?"

Wolfbane looked around. "Well, it has been puzzling me. I thought you liked to spend this part of the year in Monte Carlo."

"I do," answered Lucia. "But I've been here instead, doing some research into eighteenth-century Night Witch rituals."

"Go on," Wolfbane urged.

"It seems there was a local Night Witch in these parts called Ma Hemlock who knew a method of time travel. She's buried in the grounds of Darkwood Manor."

"And where is that?"

"A few miles along the coast at the edge of the forest. Just outside the seaside resort of Torgate. The citizens of Torgate were the ones who killed her."

"So what was her method of time travel?" Wolfbane asked impatiently.

"No one is supposed to know. Ma Hemlock took the secret to her grave," said Lucia.

Wolfbane sucked his teeth in irritation. "Well, that's no help."

Lucia nodded toward the leather-bound book on the table. "Look at the title," she instructed.

Wolfbane slid the book toward him and read out the words written in Gothic script on the cover.

"*The Journal of Matilda Hemlock*! Where did you get this?" he asked, suddenly excited.

"I found it in a junk store in Torgate," she replied. "A dreadful little man called Sid Rollin sold it to me."

Wolfbane glanced up at his mother, who was watching a fat spider slowly descending on a thread from the rafters. "Turn to page ninety-nine," she said, still watching the spider.

Wolfbane did so and with growing excitement read out the heading on the page. "How to Summon a Specter from the Nether World."

He looked up at his mother again. Then he took the spider gently into his hand, his slanting yellow eyes suddenly ablaze with malice and pleasure. "I think I'd like to have a word with Ma Hemlock, my little friend," he said softly to the spider. "Meanwhile, I need a spy in Speller."

The Time Witches

2

The Return of Captain Starlight

D espite the rain falling on Darkwood Forest, it was a perfect day in Speller. Fluffy white clouds drifted high overhead, and the sun sparkled on the dark blue sea beyond the harbor.

Abby and Spike stood on the cliff top, ready to race.

"Go!" shouted Spike, and they began to climb the same small oak tree from different sides. Spike reached the top branch first, but Abby called out, "Your side was easier."

"No way, I was faster than you," replied Spike with a grin as they looked out to sea.

A sailing ship was heading toward the harbor.

Although Spike had spent the last few weeks on vacation in Speller, where the weather was always delightful, he was as pale as ice and his fair hair almost as white as snow. Abby, on the other hand, was suntanned. She wore a red fisherman's smock and canvas shorts. Spike wore a shirt and shorts in his favorite color, dark blue.

Suddenly, the loud cry of a seabird caused them to look up. Abby's heart leaped. A great white albatross hovered above them.

"Benbow!" she shouted. "It must be Captain Starlight's boat. He's come back."

They slithered down the tree and Abby called out, "Race you to the harbor."

They ran down the path toward the town, keeping abreast. Spike shouted, "No cheating by using magic."

"I don't need to use magic," answered Abby and, with a burst of speed, she pulled slightly ahead. When they reached the first cottages, they stayed in the center of the narrow cobbled lane. There were no cars to fear in Speller. Only an occasional pedestrian watched them streak by.

Abby was still ahead as they entered the town square. With a sudden spurt, Spike caught up with her as they passed the general store run by Abby's aunt Lucy and uncle Ben. They were now in the lane that curved down to the water.

Mr. Mainbrace, the mayor, stood on the steps of the town hall and smiled as they raced past. Frowning anxiously, he said to his wife, who was taking care of the window boxes above him, "I think I'll arrange for a short, heavy shower at about nine o'clock tonight. What do you think, dearest?"

Mrs. Mainbrace considered his suggestion for a moment. "I'd make it last a full half hour. You haven't given us any rain for a few weeks. It will freshen everything up nicely for tomorrow."

The mayor smiled. "Half an hour it is."

Mr. Mainbrace tended to be a fussy man, and there was a lot to be fussy about at the moment. A great social event was about to take place in Speller, and the mayor took great pride in his civic duties.

Tomorrow, Sir Chadwick Street, Grand Master of the Ancient Order of Light Witches, would marry his betrothed,

Miss Hilda Bluebell. The couple had been staying in the town for some weeks. The wedding feast was going to be served in the square in front of the town hall, and there was still much to do before the Reverend Cannon performed the ceremony.

As Master of the Light Witches, Sir Chadwick was a great figure to be admired and the townsfolk were proud that he had chosen to be married in Speller. But they had welcomed Hilda into their hearts.

When Mrs. Porter's cow was ill from eating too many unripe apples, Hilda had stayed up all night and nursed her to health. And the day Mr. Capstan's hens had stopped laying eggs, Hilda had gone to the chicken house and had a long talk with them in their own language.

She had explained later that the chickens wanted more cuttlefish shells in their diet. After that, she could do no wrong. People would stop her in the street to pass the time of day, amazed that wherever Hilda went, she was accompanied by the sweet sound of songbirds.

When Abby and Spike had hurtled past, Mr. Mainbrace shaded his eyes with his hand and looked down into the harbor, which was clear of boats. A sleek sailing ship was running in on the turning tide. The mayor recognized the craft even though he was too far away to read the name on her prow.

"It's the *Ishmael!*" he called out with pleasure. "Captain Starlight has arrived, dearest. That's why Abby and Spike are racing to the harbor."

"Those two never need an excuse to race," replied Mrs. Mainbrace, still tending her flower boxes.

Her husband continued to watch the harbor as Abby and Spike arrived breathless on the jetty. A tall man, who had been talking with a group outside the Speller Tavern, walked across to join Abby and Spike as Captain Adam Starlight finished mooring the *Ishmael*. Starlight leaped ashore to shake the hand of his friend Sir Chadwick Street.

"Adam," Sir Chadwick said with a happy smile, "I'm delighted to see you again."

"I wouldn't want to miss your wedding, Chadwick, especially since I'm the best man," Starlight replied in a gruff New England accent. He smiled and bent to hug both Abby and Spike in his powerful arms.

Benbow, the great bird, also landed and waddled over to Abby to nuzzle his head against her leg. Abby bent down and scratched him under his beak. "Hello, old friend," she said. "Have you been looking after Captain Starlight?"

"Benbow's fine, Abby," said Starlight. "But I think he misses you sometimes."

"Come and see the others outside the Speller Tavern," said Sir Chadwick.

The captain knew the three men standing there. They were the Great Mandini; Abby's father, Harry Clover; and her uncle Ben.

"Greetings, Mandini," said Starlight as they shook hands. "Harry, Ben, good to see you. How are your wives?"

The men assured him they were fine and invited him to join them for an early lunch in the Tavern.

"Thank you, but no," Starlight answered. "I ate earlier and I want to get my legs accustomed to land. I think I'll take a stroll around the town."

"We'll come with you," chorused Abby and Spike.

"I think I'll join you, too," said Sir Chadwick.

"Are you coming, Benbow?" Starlight asked.

The albatross shook his head and hopped on board the *Ishmael*, where he made himself comfortable on a coil of rope and buried his head under his wing.

"He likes to take a nap at this time of the morning," said Starlight.

"There's been a lot of changes since you were last here, Captain," Abby told him as they walked up the cobbled hill that led to the town square.

"I thought the harbor would be much busier now the Sea Witches have resumed the Ice Dust trade," Starlight said.

"It usually is these days," Abby answered. "But they decided to moor the fleet in the lighthouse cavern to make space in the harbor for the wedding guests who are arriving by sea."

"Who are you expecting for the ceremony?" Starlight asked, waving to various townsfolk who called out greetings.

"Lots of people, old boy," Sir Chadwick replied, raising his tweed hat to three Sea Witches who were out shopping. "Light Witches from all over England," he continued. "And there's a contingent of Scottish Light Witches from the Outer Isles. The Welsh are here in strength, and a whole crowd of the Irish, complete with pookas."

"Pookas!" exclaimed Starlight. "I haven't seen a pooka in years. What kind are they?"

"A mixed bag. There's a vole, two goats, and an enormous donkey. The mayor had to ask the donkey to stay on top of the cliffs. It's so big it blocked any lane it walked down."

Starlight smiled. He knew all about pookas. They were gigantic spirit animals that sometimes chose to befriend people. Only a few human beings could see or hear them.

"Where have you put everyone?"

"On the ships in the lighthouse cavern. It was difficult for the mayor. They all started squabbling about who had the better ship to stay on. It's been a nightmare of protocol."

"What's protocol?" asked Abby.

"Conducting affairs in the proper manner so that nobody is offended," answered Spike, who was actually Altur, Prince of Lantua and Lord of the Cold Seas. "We have a lot of it in my father's palace."

The cavern Sir Chadwick had referred to was a great hidden lagoon behind a cliff that flanked Speller. It had been built by Abby's father to hide the Sea Witch fleet from the Night Witches during the recent war.

"What about the king and queen of Lantua?" Starlight asked Spike.

"They're on their way with my sister, Princess Galcia," he answered. "Luckily, my parents are traveling incognito."

"Why is that lucky?" Starlight asked, puzzled.

"Protocol again," said Spike with a shrug. "If they came as the king and queen, they'd have had to stay in a palace. Yet as the duke and duchess of Lantua, they can lodge in the rooms the mayor has prepared for them in the town hall."

Captain Starlight shook his head with a wry smile. "I'll never get used to all the playacting that goes with royalty," he said.

"Think what it's like for *me*," said Spike with feeling.

"*All the world's a stage*, Adam," said Sir Chadwick loftily, quoting Shakespeare.

"*And one man in his time plays many parts*," replied Starlight as they entered the town square. It was being decked with bunting, and an enormous tent was being erected.

Captain Starlight paused to look about him and waved to

Mr. Mainbrace, who was now helping his wife with the window boxes.

The town hall was the most imposing building in Speller. It was faced with rose-red brick trimmed with white stone and was at least three times higher than the surrounding cottages.

The only other building of such distinction was the church that had been standing close to the harbor since Saxon times. It was made of honey-colored stone. The rest of Speller consisted of pretty little whitewashed cottages. Each had a garden that grew vegetables, fruit, or grain, for the town grew all its own food.

"I haven't seen any of the children yet," said Starlight, sounding a little surprised. He had expected the streets to be full of them since they had been liberated from the Night Witches.

"They're all at choir practice with the Reverend Cannon," explained Abby. "Spike and I don't have to go because I'm a bridesmaid and he's a page."

"How are they settling down after their captivity?"

"Everybody is fine. They've even stopped having nightmares." Abby gestured toward a building with a little bell tower down one of the curving cobbled lanes. "They've reopened the school. Aunt Lucy is teaching there now."

"So, your uncle Ben is minding the store on his own."

Sir Chadwick laughed. "He says it still gives him plenty of time to practice his French horn."

"And what about you, Abby?" said Starlight.

Sir Chadwick spoke before she could answer. "Abby is doing splendidly. She's making remarkable progress in her Light Witch lessons."

"Yes," she agreed, "but I have to do twice as much home-work as anyone else."

As they stood in the square, two of the townsfolk, escorting a little cart pulled by two fine-looking pigs, stopped at the steps of the town hall. The cart was loaded with brown-paper packages.

"A consignment of Ice Dust," Sir Chadwick explained. "After it leaves the warehouse, Mr. Mainbrace inspects it. Then it's shipped to Light Witches all around the country."

Starlight gave a friendly nod to the two men with the cart. Like all the male Sea Witches of Speller, they were dressed in the traditional costume of the town: brightly colored fishermen's smocks and trousers tucked into sea boots.

The mayor began weighing the packages on a large set of brass scales. He then dripped a great blob of red sealing wax onto each and pressed the Speller town seal into the hot wax.

Ice Dust is found only in the kingdom of Lantua, a hidden country located beneath a great dome of ice in Antarctica. For a time, the Night Witches had occupied Lantua and starved the Light Witches of their supplies. And because the Night Witches couldn't survive the purity of Ice Dust, they had kidnapped the children of Speller — except for Abby — to mine it for them.

But when Abby and her friends had defeated Wolfbane and the Night Witches, they had freed the kingdom of Lantua and returned the children of Speller to their parents.

"And where does the Ice Dust go to now?" Starlight asked.

"To the Speller train station," said Abby. "If you're in the mood for a walk, Captain, I'll show you."

"Lead the way," he replied.

"We'll take this load up to the station for you, Mr. Mainbrace," Sir Chadwick volunteered.

"Thank you, Sir Chadwick," the mayor replied. "Are you sure it won't be too much trouble?"

"Not at all. We're delighted to be of service." He took the bridle of the nearside pig saying, "Trot on," and they walked up the cobbled lane that led to the top of the cliffs.

"So, what are your parents doing now that they're home?" Starlight asked Abby.

"Writing a history of Speller for the Light Witch library," she replied, pausing to pluck two apples from an overhanging branch to give to the pigs.

Sir Chadwick and Captain Starlight walked on.

"Abby isn't descended from Light Witches, is she?" asked Starlight.

Chadwick shrugged. "No, but she has Sea Witch blood. Her ancestor Jack Elvin came to Speller and opened the general store. He was a human being who worked as an engineer. Clever chap by all accounts. But his wife was a Sea Witch, and the gift appears to have come out in Abby."

"An engineer, you say?"

"That's right, and an architect. In fact, you'll see some more of his work in a moment."

They walked on up the hill, past the last of the cottages, to where the cobbled lane became a graveled pathway leading to the cliff top. From this high point, they could see the cove and the lighthouse above the great hidden lagoon where the Sea Witch fleet was anchored.

A little farther away was Darkwood Forest, partly obscured by rain clouds. Beyond that, in the far distance, was the seaside resort of Torgate. The path forked. The right fork led to the lighthouse and the left down into a tree-filled valley.

Sir Chadwick looked at Starlight. "You lived in the light-house for a time. Didn't you ever go through Jack Elvin's maze?"

Captain Starlight shook his head. "No, I arrived by sea. That's how I came and went from Speller."

"Well, this is where it gets a bit tricky," said Sir Chadwick. "We'd better wait for Abby to show us the way."

When Spike and Abby caught up, they took the path through the little forest and were suddenly all shrouded in deep shadows. The pathway cut deep into a hill and then began to turn and twist. Sometimes there was a single fork in the lane, while at other times there were several choices.

After a time, Starlight lost all sense of direction. "I'd need a compass for this route," he said. "Is it enchanted?"

"No," replied Chadwick. "That's the extraordinary thing. Jack Elvin devised it all. No magic was involved."

Abby laughed. "Do you want to know the trick of how to find your way?"

"Of course," said Starlight.

"Show him, Spike."

Spike pointed in a direction Starlight was certain led back to the cliff top. "That's the way to go."

"Are you sure it's that way, lad?" Starlight said doubtfully.

Spike nodded. "You have to take exactly the opposite direction to the one you think is correct."

"It's as simple as that?"

"Yes, that simple," said Abby. "You try, Captain. Just keep leading us in the direction you think is wrong."

Starlight followed the instruction, and after a few minutes

the path emerged from the forest and ended on the grass verge of a deserted road.

Starlight shook his head ruefully. "It's much harder than you imagine, doing what you think is the wrong thing all the time."

Sir Chadwick glanced along the road in both directions. "I'd better disguise these pigs as donkeys. We don't want any passing humans getting curious." Chadwick waved his hands and muttered an incantation.

Captain Starlight looked back the way they had just come. All he could see was what appeared to be a fringe of trees before a low cliff of sheer rock.

Suddenly, a voice with a light Irish accent said, "Did I hear someone mention a donkey?"

They looked toward the sound of the voice and slowly a vast donkey, at least the size of an elephant, materialized before them.

"Allow me to introduce myself. I'm Paddy the Pooka," the giant donkey said, and he nodded to each of them.

"Delighted to make your acquaintance," replied Chadwick warily. He knew pookas could be mischievous if they thought they had been slighted. "My name is Sir Chadwick Street, Grand Master of the Light Witches. This is Abby Clover, and Prince Altur, whom we call Spike, and lastly, Captain Adam Starlight."

"Also known as the Ancient Mariner, I believe," the pooka answered. "It's an honor to meet you fine gentlemen and you, too, Abby and Spike."

Then he looked toward the horizon. "A bus is coming, I'd better make myself smaller." There was a popping sound, and he shrunk to the normal size for a donkey.

Starlight glanced at Sir Chadwick. "I thought human beings couldn't see pookas unless the pooka wanted to reveal itself."

Paddy the Pooka answered him. "You're quite right, Captain, darlin'. But some human children have the second sight, you know."

The bus appeared over the crest of a hill from Torgate. It had once been painted bright yellow, but now it was flaking and streaked with rust. A crowd of tourists looked down from the open deck as it passed.

"Look, Mom," one boy called out. "A donkey and two pigs pulling a cart."

"No, just two donkeys, Reginald," the mother replied as the bus passed.

"I was right," Paddy said when they were alone again. "That child could see through the spell you put on the porkers." Then he reached up and placed a hoof on Sir Chadwick's shoulder. "Sure, you're a fine-looking fellow, Chaddy. Where are you off to now?"

Sir Chadwick smiled with a certain amount of discomfort. He could see Captain Starlight was enjoying the situation. "We're just going to deliver this consignment of Ice Dust to the station."

Paddy looked up at the sky and sniffed the air. "Well, it's a great day. I think I'll be coming along with you, if you don't mind?"

Sir Chadwick thought quickly. "We would be happy to have your company, Paddy, but there is a greater service you could do for us, if you would be so kind?"

"Name it, Chaddy, anything for a fine fella such as yourself."

"Could you wait here and mark the spot for the way back into Speller? It's easy to miss it if you're not careful."

"Take your time," said Paddy. "I'll be rooted to the spot while you're away."

Sir Chadwick and Captain Starlight continued with the cart. When they were out of earshot, Sir Chadwick said, "Oh, dear. I'm afraid he's taken a shine to me. Pookas are notorious for their sudden infatuations, you know. Usually they select human beings."

"He seems friendly enough," Starlight said.

"That's the problem," Sir Chadwick answered. "The trouble with pookas is they stay with you until they've performed some special favor."

"Is that so bad?" asked Starlight.

"My dear fellow," Sir Chadwick moaned. "I'm about to go on my honeymoon."

"Yes. I can see you might not want a pooka tagging along," conceded Starlight as they entered the train yard.

Why Speller had a station at all baffled anyone who took the trouble to think about it. Human beings were unaware of Speller's existence, and no one else lived nearby. The Light Witches had had the station built so they could distribute Ice Dust all around the country. Even the stationmaster was really a Sea Witch.

The little redbrick building was located on a grade crossing on the road to Torgate, where the road curved away along the coast to the nearby resort. The railway line swung out to enter a long tunnel and then pass along the other edge of Darkwood Forest before it came to Torgate.

As they entered the train yard, Captain Starlight saw there was an ancient spur line from the main railway track. It was covered with weeds and scattered about it were ancient lumps of rusting metal.

"I wonder what this was," said Spike, prodding one of the pieces of metal with his foot.

"Once upon a time, it was the *Torgate Belle*. That's all that's left of her," said a new voice. It was Mr. Reef, the stationmaster. "Good morning, Sir Chadwick," he said. "I see they've got you all working: Abby Clover, Prince Altur, *and* the Ancient Mariner."

"Quite so. Mr. Reef, have you actually been introduced to Captain Adam Starlight? He is going to be my best man."

"Delighted, sir," replied Mr. Reef. Then he looked toward Spike who was still examining the rusting lumps of metal. "I see you're interested in the remains of the *Torgate Belle*."

"How long has it been here, Mr. Reef?" asked Spike.

"At least since my father's time," he replied. "He was stationmaster before me. When the *Torgate Belle* was wrecked, the railway company dumped what was left of her here."

Starlight, Abby, and Spike continued to examine the ancient remains of the train while Sir Chadwick handed over all the packages to Mr. Reef. They then led the empty cart back to the entrance of Jack Elvin's maze.

There was no sign of Paddy the Pooka. "He seems to have forgotten us," Starlight said as they left the road. Sir Chadwick nodded. "Pookas have a very low boredom threshold. I only hope he's found someone else on whom to lavish his affections."

"Better keep your fingers crossed," said Starlight.

"I would look absurd," said Sir Chadwick. "The Grand Master of Light Witches with his fingers crossed for good luck."

A few minutes later, they had made their way through the maze and descended the cobbled lane into Speller.

3

Abby's New Feat of Magic

Abby and Spike stayed in the town square while Sir Chadwick and Captain Starlight returned the pig cart to the little warehouse near the harbor. They wanted to watch a crew of Sea Witches finish erecting the giant tent that would hold all the guests for the wedding feast.

Because the Sea Witches could control the weather, there was no fear of rain for the great occasion. The mighty tent was to provide shade rather than shelter.

Abby admired the way the great poles were hoisted into place and how casually the Sea Witches ran up and down the rigging to secure the massive spread of blue-and-white striped canvas overhead.

Coming from the church was the sound of the other children of Speller rehearsing a wedding song under the direction of the Reverend Cannon.

As they continued to watch, Samuel Porter, one of the Sea Witches working in the top rigging of the tent, called down to Spike, "Bring up that rope by your feet, lad."

Spike picked up the end of the rope, tucked it into his belt, and was about to start climbing the rigging when Abby stopped him. "Just hold onto it tightly, Spike." She took hold of the rope herself and muttered an incantation:

"Rope to go higher,
You will aspire."

The rope uncoiled and lifted them both through the air until they let go and stepped onto the pole where Sam was working.

Sam laughed. "You and your tricks, Abby Clover. But I've seen that one before."

"Where, Sam?"

"In India, but the boy who did it vanished when he got to the top."

"Like this?" said Abby, whistling a little tune that Captain Starlight had once taught her. She disappeared.

Sam laughed again. "All right, young lady, that's enough of your Light Witch ways. I've got work to do."

Abby whistled the tune again, this time in reverse, and reappeared. "Come on, Spike," she said and, taking hold of the rope, she slid to the ground. Spike followed, and they strolled from the tent and stood in the cobbled lane that led down to the harbor.

"Why don't the Sea Witches just use magic to put up the tent, Abby?" Spike asked.

Abby shrugged. "They don't use magic much, only to navigate the oceans and control the weather. They gave up most of it years ago when they became seafarers."

"Is learning magic very hard work?" Spike asked as they walked down the hill.

Abby sighed. "I should say so, you should see the home-work I have to do."

"What have you learned? Can you show me anything new?"

Abby thought for a moment. "Mostly history and lists of things to learn. But I can do this now — Light Witches call it tobbing."

Abby pointed across the street. "You see the pear tree in Mr. Cable's garden?"

Spike looked at the tree and saw Abby sitting on one of its lower branches.

"Gosh," he said, impressed. Abby threw a pear down to him, then reappeared at his side. "Can you take yourself any-where by doing that?"

Abby shook her head. "No, only to places I can see. Sir Chadwick says that one day I might be able to take myself any-where. But only very powerful Light Witches can do that."

"It sounds more fun than being a prince," Spike said with a sigh.

"Don't you like being a prince, Spike?"

"It's all right, but it's not much fun."

"What do you actually have to do?"

"Be wise, be kind, think of your people before yourself," Spike said as if he were chanting a multiplication table. "At least that's what my father says. But all I have to do is dress up in various uniforms and open things, or inspect good works when my father is too busy to do it himself."

"No wonder you like coming here on vacation."

Spike nodded his head vigorously. "You bet I do," he replied with feeling. Then, looking thoughtful, he added, "Do you realize I've been here nearly two weeks, and we haven't been out in the Atlantis Boat once?"

"The boat's been away," Abby said.

"Away?" repeated Spike, puzzled.

"Yes," Abby said. "It takes itself off sometimes."

"Where does it go?"

"I've no idea. I asked my dad. He thinks it goes away to learn things."

Spike thought about this for a moment. "I would have thought it knew enough already," he said eventually.

"Me, too," Abby said. "It really is full of surprises."

The Atlantis Boat was a wonderful craft, discovered by Captain Starlight and Abby's parents a long time ago. Its engines worked on salt, and it could go underwater, fly, and travel at astonishing speeds. The Atlanteans, who were star voyagers, had left it on Earth. Even now, Abby didn't know all of the feats the little boat was capable of.

Suddenly, a white flash passed overhead.

Just then the town hall clock began to chime eleven. "Oh, dear," Abby said, sounding concerned. "I'm supposed to be at home for a fitting of my bridesmaid's dress." She gave a long call. "Benbow!"

The huge albatross now circling above them swooped down in a long, curving dive and hovered over their heads.

"Will you take me to the lighthouse, please, Benbow?" Abby said and reached up to take hold of his feet.

"I'm going for a swim," Spike said. "Can he give me a lift, too?"

"Grab hold of a foot," said Abby.

"Benbow," Spike called out. "Please will you drop me in the sea in front of the lighthouse?"

Benbow gave a squawk and came lower so that Spike could also take hold.

Now the great bird soared into the air, carrying the children over the town and into the next bay.

While they were still over the water, Spike called out, "See you later," and let go. Abby watched as he splashed into the sea and disappeared beneath the waves.

Benbow carried Abby until she could drop gently onto the observation platform of the lighthouse where she lived. She paused for a moment and looked out to sea where Spike was swimming in the bay. She saw the flash of a dolphin's back as it played with him.

Already Benbow was skimming over the waves above Spike and his companion. Abby felt a sting of envy as she descended to face the tedium of her dress fitting.

4

Sid Rollin Finds a Willing Customer

In Torgate, along the coast from Speller, Sid Rollin stood at the window of his real estate agent's office and watched the pelting rain, blown almost horizontal by a gusting wind, splashing onto the promenade.

"Another perfect day in England's premier seaside resort," he muttered bitterly.

A few misguided tourists hurried along the pavement. Others stood beneath the bus shelter in front of the floral clock, gazing miserably at the drab gray sea. Litter whirled along the promenade. Hamburger wrappers and used paper cups clogged the gutters.

The empty hamburger wrappers were the only thing about the view that gave Sid Rollin any pleasure. He owned the bar next door that sold them. He also owned the real estate agency, the butcher shop, and many of the other businesses in Torgate.

Despite the awful weather, Mr. Rollin was dressed for a warm Victorian summer's day. He wore a cream-and-scarlet striped blazer, tightly stretched across his ample stomach. A straw boater was perched at a jaunty angle on his head, and baggy white-flannel trousers sagged over his grubby tennis shoes.

The chamber of commerce had decided that all store owners in Torgate should wear clothes that encouraged visitors to believe they were staying in a festive seaside town. But, somehow, the effect served only to emphasize the depressing nature of the rundown resort.

The tide was now on the ebb and Sid Rollin could see a long stretch of the beach. It was pebbled with sharp flinty stones and merged grayly with the sullen sea that reached out to the horizon.

Also revealed by the outgoing tide were two rows of blackened stumps coated with seaweed and encrusted with barnacles. Once, long ago, they had supported Torgate Pier.

Coming from the fair, a few yards from his shop, Sid could hear an out-of-tune pipe organ playing "Oh, We Do Like to Be Beside the Seaside." A view evidently not shared by the gloomy-looking tourists Sid could see from his window.

He sighed, slumped down at his desk, and looked at a Victorian poster for Torgate on the opposite wall. It showed quite another world.

In the picture, sunshine shone from a cloudless sky on to a promenade that was decked with hanging baskets of flowers. The fair was bright with dazzling colors, instead of the dull, chipped paint and rusty superstructures that marred the attractions of the present day.

In the poster, the Pavilion Theater, with its onion-shaped towers, stood at the end of the pier crowded with happy people. More crowds thronged the golden sands that sloped gently to a sparkling blue sea.

Sid Rollin knew why things had changed so dramatically in Torgate. More than a hundred years ago, a great storm had devastated the town. In one terrible night, the storm had blown down the pier and washed up great deposits of sharp flint stones to cover the golden sands. Anyone unwise enough to walk along the seashore now could only do so wearing a thick pair of boots as protection against the cutting pebbles.

Sid looked at the calendar on his desk and studied the date he had ringed with a red pencil. Three more weeks until his own vacation, when he would escape from Torgate for a few precious days.

As he looked up, he started in surprise. A man stood before him, but Sid had not heard him enter the shop. The man wore a wide-brimmed black hat and a dripping raincoat. It was Wolfbane, carrying his suitcase.

"Good morning, sir," Sid said automatically as he recovered from his shock. "How may I help you?"

Wolfbane smiled, but the thin cruel face did not look any more pleasant. Sid thought the mysterious-looking man must have been staying in Torgate for some time, judging by his papery white complexion.

"I'd like to rent premises on the seafront. Somewhere near the floral clock would be ideal," Wolfbane said. His voice was soft and cultivated, but his breath smelled like sulfur.

He must have been eating one of my hamburgers, Rollin thought. There had been several complaints about their dreadful effects at the last council meeting. He stood up and held out his hand. "You've come to the right place, sir. Sid Rollin is my name. Torgate's one and only real estate agent."

"Delighted," said the figure, ignoring Sid's hand. "My name is Mr. Wolfbane. I have a further request."

"Name it," said Sid. "My aim is to please."

"I have a particular medical condition," Wolfbane continued. "I must be careful what businesses were previously conducted on the premises I rent in case of allergies. Do you have complete records of all earlier occupants?"

Rollin gestured toward a row of filing cabinets. "Everything is here, sir, going back to the year one. All anyone would want to know about one of our properties."

"With your permission," said Wolfbane, opening a drawer. His hands flickered through the files at incredible speed. Finally, he extracted one and muttered to himself as he read the contents. "Unoccupied throughout the summer of 1894. Excellent! This one will do splendidly."

"The old ice-cream parlor, sir." Rollin took a large bunch of keys from a drawer and an umbrella from a stand in the corner. "Would you like to leave your bag here? It'll be quite safe."

"I prefer to keep it with me," Wolfbane replied, following Sid into the street. They only had to walk a few yards before Sid Rollin stopped in front of a neglected-looking shop. The faded sign above the door said DELLA FRANCESCA ICE CREAM PARLOR, but the windows were covered with a thick layer of posters.

Inside the shop, everything was coated in a layer of dust. There were a few broken chairs by a splintered counter and an old sign listing various delectable ice-cream concoctions once served in the shop.

"There's a good-sized basement down here," Sid said, leading Wolfbane to the staircase at the rear of the shop.

"It could do with a good cleaning, of course," Rollin said hastily when they stood in the damp cellar.

Wolfbane placed his suitcase on the floor and, looking at the fungus-covered walls, smiled again. "Perfect," he said, and Sid Rollin just managed to turn away to avoid Wolfbane's breath.

"Should I arrange for cleaning?" Sid asked.

Wolfbane shook his head. "No, Mr. Rollin. But let's get back to your office. You might be able to give me some further information."

In the pelting rain, they hurried back toward the real estate agent's office.

"Anything I can do to help, Mr. Wolfbane," Sid answered, unable to conceal his delight at getting the dreadful shop off his books.

"I understand there is a rather large house on the outskirts of the town. Do you know the property?"

Sid nodded. "You must mean Darkwood Manor. It's the only house of any distinction near Torgate."

"How do I get there?"

Once inside his office, Rollin took a map of Torgate from his inside pocket and, turning his head slightly to avoid Wolfbane's dreadful breath, showed him the exact location.

"Splendid," said Wolfbane, producing a checkbook. "Please tell me what I owe you."

Sid Rollin licked his lips as Wolfbane wrote out the amount.

Handing him the check, Wolfbane smiled and said, "What a perfect day it's turning out to be."

"Not bad at all," muttered Sid Rollin, smiling smugly at the rain as he fingered Wolfbane's check in his pocket.

The Time Witches

5

Wolfbane Casts
an Evil Spell

When he left the real estate agent's office, Wolfbane returned to the old ice-cream parlor and locked the door. Then he took stock of his new premises. In the rooms above, he found a small kitchen and in one of the closets a large empty glass jar at least the size of a dustbin. Excellent, he muttered to himself, carrying the huge storage jar down to the dank basement. He placed it carefully in a corner.

After unpacking his suitcase, he took a bag of Black Dust and poured a small amount into the jar. Then, opening the first of two small boxes, he added a tiny amount of the mauve-colored Bigger Powder his mother had given him. He opened the second box and removed a wriggling spider, which he added to the contents of the mixture he had prepared.

Now he examined the damp brick floor of the basement. Scraping a space in the layer of old newspapers and cardboard boxes that littered the room, he drew a large star with a piece of chalk, adding various ancient symbols at the points. Then he placed the large jar in the center.

Standing back to admire his work, he took a pin from the lapel of his jacket and pricked his thumb. Blood welled from the tiny wound, and he dripped three large drops into the jar before sealing it shut.

"Ready," he said aloud, taking a robe from the open suitcase and draping it about his shoulders. Although the air in the basement was quite still, the black material swirled about his body as if blown by the wind. As the cloak moved about Wolfbane's body, strange images appeared in the flowing material: demons, reptiles, and savage animals. He began to chant.

"Demons and devils be my friend,
Princes of darkness will you send
Evil powers that I need
To make my devilish plan succeed."

As he chanted, the contents of the large old jar began to glow a dark purplish color. Wolfbane finished his incantation and nodded with satisfaction. He removed his robe, locked it in the suitcase, and left the shop.

It was still drizzling rain on the litter-strewn seafront, and a chilling wind blew along the promenade. Wolfbane consulted the map Sid Rollin had given him and decided he would take a taxi.

He walked to Torgate station and found one rust-streaked cab out front. A sly-looking youth wearing a baseball cap sat at the wheel eating a hamburger. Its nauseating smell filled the cab as Wolfbane slid into the back seat.

"Where to, sir?" the youth asked in a familiar manner.

"Darkwood Manor," Wolfbane answered curtly from the backseat. "And I will need you to wait."

"Do you want the scenic route or should we go along the promenade?" the youth said with a snicker.

"The fastest way — and less talking," Wolfbane snarled. The youth tugged the peak of his cap and roared away, tires squealing on the wet asphalt.

The taxi reached the edge of the town and passed by a road of scruffy bungalows. The road began to climb, running parallel to the cliff tops overlooking the sea. To the right lay a scrubby wasteland that marked the beginning of Darkwood Forest.

As the wasteland became more heavily wooded, Wolfbane saw a high wall of blackened bricks. The youth turned off the road and passed through a pair of open iron gates into a long driveway. The car had to slow down to avoid the many rain-filled potholes.

Eventually, the taxi came to a halt next to a decrepit, dried-out fountain in front of the manor house. Wolfbane got out of the taxi and stood for a moment, looking around. Although the rain had stopped, water still dripped from the gnarled old trees that surrounded and overhung the house.

The style of the building was Elizabethan. It must have been at least five hundred years old. Moss grew on the sagging roof, and ivy had spread in choking profusion over the front of the house. When the taxi engine was turned off, the only sound was of constant dripping and the melancholy crying of a colony of rooks in the trees.

Wolfbane found a bellpull next to the door and yanked it hard. He could hear the distant ringing. After a minute, the door creaked open and a suspicious-looking old man, dressed as a butler, peered out at him. "No solicitors," he barked.

Wolfbane fixed him with a haughty glare and replied, "Tell your master I bring news of something that could be of great advantage to him."

The butler sniffed and said, "Wait here."

After a few minutes, he returned and opened the door wider. "Lord Darkwood says you're to wait in the library. This way." He led Wolfbane through a vast hall that was decorated with suits of armor and the stuffed heads of stags, and into a large gloomy room filled with shelves lined with crumbling books. The old butler indicated a chair with torn upholstery next to the cold fireplace and tottered away.

A few minutes later, a short, bald man with an angry brick-red face entered the room. Wolfbane stood up and extended a hand, but the man kept his own hands buried in the pockets of a mud-colored tweed suit.

"Who are you and what do you want?" he demanded.

"Lord Darkwood, allow me to introduce myself. My name is Wolfbane. I am from the National Association for the Preservation of Historic Buildings. I am here to assess whether Darkwood Manor is eligible for a restoration grant."

"Restoration grant — how much?" Lord Darkwood grunted.

Wolfbane saw the sudden interest in the old man's eyes. He looked around him and said, "Well, the amount for the last building of this quality we restored came to several hundred thousand pounds."

"Several hundred thousand pounds!" gasped Lord Darkwood. He immediately became suspicious. "What would I have to do for that?"

"Nothing, really," said Wolfbane smoothly. "We would want to take some photographs for the national archives when the work is completed. That's all."

"And who does the work?" snapped Lord Darkwood.

"I'm afraid you would have to arrange that. We'd decide on the amount needed. Then we'd give you the money so that you could get the improvements done at your convenience."

A slow smile began to spread across Lord Darkwood's fiery features. "Well, that all sounds satisfactory. What do I do now?"

"If you could show me around the house and the estate, my lord, I'll be able to complete my report," Wolfbane said, smiling.

"Delighted, delighted," said Darkwood, rubbing his hands together. "Where would you like to start, in the house or out on the grounds?"

Wolfbane hesitated. "I understand there is a grave somewhere on the estate that may be of historic interest."

Lord Darkwood wrinkled his brow for a moment. "Grave, grave? All the Darkwoods are in the family vault below stairs." Then his brow cleared. "Oh, you probably mean the Witch Tree. That's only a legend, you know. But I can show you where it grows."

"If you would," Wolfbane said with a slight bow and a satisfied smile.

Lord Darkwood led him from the house and through the neglected gardens behind it. They passed a weed-filled ornamental lake and eventually came to a small forest within the walls of the estate. In the center was a clearing, and Lord Darkwood stopped in the middle before a curiously gnarled and twisted tree that was heavy with dark, fleshy leaves.

"This must be what you mean," he said, slapping the trunk of the tree. "Legend has it that the townsfolk complained of a witch in Torgate. That was sometime in the eighteenth century. My ancestor was the local magistrate. He had her dunked in the lake over there," Darkwood said, indicating with his thumb.

"Did she drown?" Wolfbane asked.

Darkwood shook his head. "No, the story says she survived, so they burned her on this spot." He looked at the tree again. "Then this thing grew here."

"What species is it?"

Darkwood shook his head. "That's the strange part. No one has ever seen this kind of tree before. In my father's day, they had some people down from Kew Gardens to look at it. They left completely baffled."

Wolfbane nodded. "Well, if the tree is that rare, it certainly must be preserved. Perhaps we can see the rest of the estate now, my lord?"

"Of course," Darkwood said, and they strolled back to the house.

Starting with the attic, Lord Darkwood took Wolfbane through each floor, until finally they reached the vast stone cellar beneath the building.

"This cellar was part of the original castle that stood here," Darkwood explained, slapping his hand against the bars of an iron cage set against the stone wall. "They pulled it down in Elizabethan times and built the manor house, but they kept the dungeons."

Wolfbane examined one of the iron cages. "And I see they still work."

"Oh, yes."

Wolfbane looked about him with a contented expression. "I imagine there is a lot of work involved in the house. Lady Darkwood must be kept very busy."

"Lady Darkwood?" His Lordship repeated. "There is no Lady Darkwood. Just myself and Jorrocks, the butler. This is a bachelor establishment, sir."

"Quite so," said Wolfbane. "Would you mind if I called Jorrocks? Oh, and the young man who is waiting in the taxi outside?"

"As you wish," said Darkwood, anxious now to please his guest. When Jorrocks and the driver had joined them, Wolfbane took a camera from his pocket. "Would you all be so kind as to step inside this cage with Lord Darkwood, gentlemen?"

"What's this for, sir?" the driver asked.

"I wish to take a picture for my report. Your presence will give it scale."

"Will I get paid extra?" the youth asked as he stepped into the iron cage along with Lord Darkwood and Jorrocks.

"No," replied Wolfbane turning the key, then putting it in his pocket. "But I promise I'll devise some interesting form of torture to repay you for your insolence."

Wolfbane turned away and strolled in the direction of the stairs, ignoring the shouts of his captives.

When he had shut the door behind him and stood in the great hall again, he stopped and listened. "Not a sound to be heard," he muttered with approval. "They don't make dungeons of that quality these days." He threw off his raincoat to reveal the swirling dark robe beneath and stood in the center of the hall. Raising his arms he shouted, *"Horribus!"*

At his call, all the windows of the manor house flew open. Taking a wand from his belt he chanted:

"Children of darkness, come to me,
All Night Witches let there be."

After a few moments, the air filled with a sound like the beating wings of a flock of giant birds. Then, fluttering through the open windows came clusters of Night Witches. With their cloaks attached to their hands and feet, they looked like a colony of giant bats.

6

Mary Bowsprit's Diary

After Benbow landed her on top of the lighthouse, Abby hurried down to the living room. It was a big circular space, with white stone walls. Captain Starlight had once lived there for a time. In those days, it had been done up like a ship's cabin. There were still some of his sea chests against the walls and a great chair made out of old sea-smoothed driftwood.

The room was full today. Aunt Lucy was delving into a sewing box. Standing on the large round table in the center of the room was Hilda Bluebell in her wedding dress. Abby's mother, Madge Clover, was pinning up the hem.

Abby's father, Harry, sat at the other end of the table with a pile of documents before him. He was making notes in a large folder, but he looked up at Abby and winked. He had a study below, but he often preferred to work in the living room.

Abby never cared much about her own appearance, but she thought Hilda looked lovely. The white material of the dress seemed to glow gently as it swirled about her, and the veil was secured to her golden hair with clusters of tiny white flowers.

"Gosh, you look beautiful, Hilda," Abby said. "No wonder Sir Chadwick wants to marry you."

Hilda smiled, but there was a hint of anxiety in her eyes.

Abby's mother found a loose thread that she absentmindedly tried to snap with her hands. She stopped and shook her head. "I keep forgetting it's made of fairy thread. Where are those scissors that came with the material?"

Abby found a small pair of silver scissors on the table and handed them to her mother. When she'd snipped through the thread, Madge said, "I still find it amazing that you can't cut through this thread with a carving knife yet these scissors slice through the cloth so easily."

"Fairy thread is the strongest stuff you can imagine," Abby explained. "I had to make some once, it took ages."

Hilda looked down. "The fairies of the Outer Islands made

the material and the thread as a present," she said. "They made the scissors as well. Sadly, they're too shy to come to the wedding."

"Gosh," said Abby, "I'd like to see a fairy."

"Well, it's a good thing they sent the scissors, otherwise it would have been impossible to do this job," exclaimed Abby's mother, snipping off another loose thread. Then she stood back and looked at her handiwork.

"What do you think, Harry?" she asked her husband.

He looked up from his papers and studied Hilda. "You've done a magnificent job," he replied. "Hilda, you look like a princess."

Hilda gave a worried smile. "I don't feel like one," she said ruefully. "I don't feel at all worthy of Chadwick."

"That's nonsense," Madge Clover said firmly. "Chadwick is a lucky man to be getting a wife like you — and he knows it."

"But he is the Grand Master of Light Witches, and his family is so rich," Hilda continued. "I'm just an orphan from Torgate."

"I didn't know you came from Torgate, Hilda," said Abby.

"Oh, yes," Hilda replied. "It's a coincidence that I'm getting married so close to where I lived as a child."

"I've been there a couple of times," said Abby. "It's a bit dreary."

"It used to be lovely," replied Hilda. "But I hear it's changed since I was a girl."

"It must have been hard being an orphan."

Hilda looked down. "It wasn't so bad. But it doesn't make you feel very important in life."

"It's what you are in your heart that counts, Hilda," Aunt Lucy said briskly.

Hilda smiled, but Abby could see she still wasn't con-vinced.

"Down you come," Madge said. "It's Abby's turn to be fit-ted now."

Hilda stepped from the table and floated gently down to stand on the floor. Madge leaned forward and kissed her on the forehead. "You'll be the prettiest girl in Speller when you walk back down the aisle on your husband's arm tomorrow," she said. "Now, go and hang the dress up in your bedroom." Then to Abby she said, "Up you go, young lady."

Abby sighed and took the place vacated by Hilda. After only a few minutes of her fitting, she began to wriggle.

"Stand still," ordered her mother.

Abby sighed again. "You know, Captain Starlight used to design ships for the Light Witches of Bright Town in Massa-chusetts," she said. "When he'd done a drawing, the Light Witches just used magic to build the ships. Why don't we do the same with my dress?"

Madge Clover laughed. "Some things are worth working for, Abby. If they come too easy, there's no pleasure in them."

Abby hung her head gloomily. "That's what Sir Chadwick always says. Sometimes I don't understand grown-ups."

"Well, magic isn't everything," Madge said.

Abby stood quietly for a while and then said, "Dad."

"Yes?" Harry Clover replied, looking up from his heap of documents.

"Could anyone else in our family do magic?"

Harry Clover shook his head. "No one on my side of the family. Your ancestor who first settled in Speller was an engi-neer and an architect from the north of England. He certainly wasn't a witch."

"Tell me again how he came to live in Speller," said Abby.

"He came at the same time as the elves came to Darkwood Forest, so the story goes," said Aunt Lucy as she brushed some threads from the table.

"He built the town hall," added Madge. "And the maze. And that was before he opened the store."

"Is that all we know about him?" asked Abby.

"Not all," replied Harry Clover. "Your mother found this in the store." He held up a fat red book. "It's the diary of Mary Bowsprit, another one of your ancestors."

"What does it say?" asked Abby, excited by the discovery. Her father opened the pages and read aloud.

"June 17, 1894. Today, my father, Josiah Bowsprit, met a human being at the Railway Station, just as the eleven o'clock train to Torgate was due. His name is Jack Elvin. The wheel to my father's wagon had come off and Mr. Elvin helped him with the repairs. Father brought him into town.

"There is much excitement in Speller because he is the first human being we have ever seen. He is a fine-looking young man with green eyes and a bold and merry smile."

Harry closed the book. "Mary must have liked him a lot because she became your great-great-grandmother."

"So Mary was a Sea Witch," Abby said. "That's where my magic must come from."

"All done," said Madge suddenly.

Abby quickly wriggled out of the dress. "May I go now?" she asked. "I want to go swimming with Spike."

"Be back in time for supper," Madge called as Abby dashed from the room.

Aunt Lucy thought for a moment while she wiped her hands on her apron. "I seem to remember that Jack Elvin had another name before he came to Speller," she said to her sister.

Madge nodded. "Yes, that rings a bell with me, too."

Harry Clover was gathering the papers to return them to his study. As he picked up the red diary, a piece of folded paper slid out from between the last pages. It was an ancient theater playbill. Harry read it aloud:

"The Pavilion Theater, Torgate, presents:
The Pavilion Players in a one-act melodrama.
Followed by a song and a smile from
Charles Stanhope and Mary Goodheart
Pat O'Grass and His Dancing Leprechauns
Dickie Richards, the King of Laughter
The Amazing Chedgey, Master of Illusion
Wo Ching with fire and sword
And the Torgate Serenaders.
Tonight at 8 o'clock."

"I wonder why Mary Bowsprit kept this?" Harry said as he tucked the old playbill back into the diary.

The Time Witches

7

The Arrival of the
King and Queen
of Lantua

Abby stood on the balcony of the lighthouse and called to Benbow who was circling overhead. She could see Spike still swimming with the dolphins in the bay.

When Benbow swooped down to allow Abby to grasp his legs, she whistled the strange little tune Captain Starlight had taught her. As she and Benbow soared above the bay, they both vanished from sight.

"Softly, Benbow. Let's give Spike a surprise," she whispered to the albatross. The great bird slowed the beating of his wings, and they made a silent descent to where Spike was cavorting in the water with the two dolphins.

As Benbow and Abby hovered silent and invisible above Spike, Abby could hear him talking to the dolphins in the language of the sea. She only understood a few of the curious clicking and whistling sounds, but Spike had always been able to chat effortlessly to the circling creatures.

Suddenly, Abby let go of Benbow's legs. As the bird reappeared, Abby, still invisible, splashed into the sea next to Spike. The dolphins raised themselves half out of the water and squeaked in astonishment, but Spike pretended he wasn't surprised.

"Come out, Abby Clover, wherever you are," he shouted.

Abby whistled her tune in reverse and appeared beside him.

Spike continued his conversation with the dolphins for another minute or so, then they flicked their tails and sped off out to sea.

"What did they say?" Abby asked, treading water.

"My parents will be here within the hour," Spike answered, grinning. "The royal yacht is just over the horizon."

"Race you to the harbor," Abby challenged and swam off as fast as she could toward Speller. Abby was a strong swimmer, but the sea was a second home to Spike and he could always outpace her in the water.

"It's not fair," said Abby as they reached the entrance of the harbor. "No matter how hard I try, you're always faster than I am."

"That's because I'm Lord of the Cold Seas and you're only a duchess," Spike answered as they pulled themselves from the water and up on to the jetty next to Captain Starlight's boat, *Ishmael*.

"Well, I don't feel like a duchess, even though your father did make me one," said Abby.

Dripping seawater, they padded along the harbor wall. A familiar group was standing in the sunshine outside the Speller Tavern: Uncle Ben, Sir Chadwick, the Great Mandini, and Captain Starlight.

All but Starlight had just come from the town tailor. They were wearing the clothes he had made them for the wedding, which they thought would also be appropriate for greeting the king and queen of Lantua. Captain Starlight was in his dress uniform: a braided cap, dark blue jacket with gold buttons and epaulets, and trousers with a wide gold stripe down them. His dress shoes had gold buckles and shone bright black. He held a gleaming ceremonial telescope under his arm.

The others wore traditional morning dress, as was proper for a wedding, but each had chosen differently. The Great Mandini had decided on a scarlet frock coat, crossed with the pale blue ribbon of Admiral of the Imperial Fleet of Lantua, a decoration awarded to him by Spike's father for his role in the destruction of the Night Witches' Shark Boat armada. His top hat sported a large scarlet peacock feather.

Uncle Ben's morning dress and top hat were in dark blue silk. Only Sir Chadwick was dressed with classical precision: black top hat, black frock coat, striped trousers, a perfectly tied silver cravat at his throat, and a gold watch chain across his black waistcoat. A blue cornflower was in his buttonhole.

Abby called out, "A dolphin told Spike that the royal yacht of Lantua is just over the horizon."

"I'll get ready," replied the Great Mandini. With a sweeping flourish, he produced two red-and-yellow flags and began to signal to a battery of cannons mounted on the cliff tops above Speller.

Captain Starlight snapped open his telescope and saw that Reverend Cannon, who was in charge of the guns, was returning his signal. "Sails in sight," he read out. "Await your order to commence firing salute."

Just then the mayor came hurrying down the street, still adjusting his heavy chain of office. A great crowd was following at a more leisurely pace.

First in the procession were the senior Light Witches who had been invited to the wedding. Abby knew from experience that Light Witches could be a touchy crowd, prone to extravagance and showiness in their general dress and demeanor. Today, with royalty expected, they lived up to their reputation.

Most Light Witches were connected in one way or another to the theater. Sir Chadwick Street, who was a great Shakespearean actor, owned the Alhambra Theater in London, and Hilda Bluebell also acted in its company.

Abby had never seen such a fantastic collection of individuals as the Light Witches.

Originally, Light Witches had worn long white robes for special ceremonies. But over the centuries, they had gradually adapted the robes to suit their individual styles. So, although their garments were still white, each dressed according to his or her favorite period of history.

Abby saw a sprinkling of Roman togas, one or two Vikings, medieval noblemen, Regency bucks, and ladies in eighteenth-century court dress. Others wore great wigs and crinolines from the Restoration period. Victorian ladies and gentlemen were there, Edwardian dandies, and even flappers from the 1920s. Mingling among them were the Irish pookas.

Sir Chadwick was looking at them a bit anxiously when he heard a voice at his shoulder.

"I'm here, Chaddy, m'boy," said Paddy the Pooka, who was still the normal size for a donkey. "Did you think I'd forgotten you?"

Sir Chadwick smiled thinly and said, "Nice to see you again, Paddy."

"Now isn't this a great sight?" said Paddy. "And just look at those townsfolk. They certainly know how to put on a show of welcome."

Following the Light Witches were the citizens of Speller,

led by the town band playing the "Sea Witch Hornpipe." The townsfolk, dressed in their traditional clothes of many colors, danced their way down to the harbor.

Just then a fabulous creature, the size of a fishing boat, surfaced in the harbor and blew out a high fountain of water. It was Princess Galcia's serpent, a wonderful mechanical toy that looked like a dragon and shone like silver in the bright sunlight. Then the royal yacht entered the harbor.

The Great Mandini gave his signal, and the cannons above the town roared out a five-gun salute. "Only five guns for a king?" said the mayor anxiously. "Is that correct?"

The Great Mandini waved a hand. "The king is traveling incognito, Your Worship. That is the proper salute for the grand duke of Lantua. Remember, he and the queen are each to be addressed as Your Grace, not Your Royal Highness."

"Of course," said the mayor, flustered. "It slipped my mind for a moment."

In all the excitement, Abby had forgotten that she and Spike were still dripping wet. "We're soaked," she whispered to Spike. "What will your parents think?"

"Don't worry," he hissed. "Royalty are trained not to notice things they don't want to see." Spike took her hand and hurried forward to where the gangplank had been put in place.

Although the king and queen of Lantua were not wearing crowns, they looked very regal. The queen wore a very smart cream-colored silk suit and a sun hat with a wide brim. The king was dressed in the light blue uniform of the Imperial Lantua Guards. Princess Galcia, in a summer dress, stood behind her parents and forgot protocol for a moment to wave to her brother and Abby.

Spike stepped forward and said with a bow, "I trust you had

a pleasant voyage, sir." Abby was always slightly surprised to hear how formally Spike spoke to his parents when there were other people about. "You may remember my friend, Abby Clover?"

The king now smiled. "How could we ever forget the duchess of the Cold Seas? The royal family of Lantua owe her a debt that can never be repaid."

"May I present Mr. Mainbrace, the mayor of Speller," Spike continued. "Mr. Mainbrace, the grand duke and duchess of Lantua."

Mr. Mainbrace bowed and said, "Welcome to Speller, Your Majes — I mean Your Graces."

Then the others pressed forward and the king and queen of Lantua were shaking hands with Sir Chadwick, Captain Starlight, and the Great Mandini, chatting like old friends.

After a while, Mr. Mainbrace suggested to Spike, "Perhaps Their Graces would like to see their quarters?"

The king overheard his query and said, "Lead on, my dear fellow."

The royal party made slow progress toward the town hall, led by the band playing a selection of sea shanties.

The king and queen, flanked by Sir Chadwick and the mayor, followed. The Light Witches hurried after them, jostling to be nearest to the royal party until Sir Chadwick turned and gave them a warning frown.

"How delightful it is here, my dear," said the king to the queen as they passed through the narrow cobbled lanes and the whitewashed houses with their fragrant gardens. "The air is so pure."

The queen nodded. "I love our kingdom, but it is nice to see the sun shining occasionally."

In Lantua, they lived beneath a great dome of ice on the continent of Antarctica.

The king suddenly stopped. The Light Witches, taken by surprise, stumbled into one another. "I have a wonderful idea," said the king.

"Yes, darling," replied the queen.

Abby was surprised to hear the queen sound so affectionate in public.

"Why don't we have a summer place here in Speller?" The king seized the arm of the mayor. "What do you think of that, Mr. Mainbrace?"

The mayor was confused by the request. On the one hand, it would be a great honor, but to build a palace would totally change the character of the town.

Spike immediately understood his dilemma and spoke out. "Perhaps a large building would be out of keeping in Speller. Don't you think, Father?" he added quickly.

The king shook his head. "Oh, I was thinking of just having a little cottage. After all, we would be incognito. No fuss, no uniforms." He stopped by a garden where pigs lolled contentedly in fresh lavender-scented hay and ducks quacked as they paddled about on a little pond.

"What magnificent creatures," said the king. As he inhaled, he looked puzzled. "These pigs smell of fresh heather," he said. "How can that be?"

"They're a special breed called Sweet Pinkies, Father," explained Spike. "They don't smell like other pigs."

"Splendid," said the King. "We'll purchase a small cottage here, and I will raise Sweet Pinkies."

The townsfolk gave a cheer of approval, and the party moved on to the town hall.

When the royal couple reached the top of the flight of steps, the king turned to address the crowd.

"Dear friends, Light Witches, distinguished pookas, and citizens of Speller. My wife and I are deeply touched by your kind reception. But we must not forget the purpose of our visit to your fair town.

"We are here to attend the wedding of our dear and trusted friend Sir Chadwick Street, to the maiden Hilda Blue-bell. This is a great occasion for them, and they are the most important people at these celebrations.

"Therefore, my wife and I beseech you not to treat us as royalty but just as you would any other grand duke and duchess you might meet on the streets of Speller."

"What a darlin' fella," shouted out Paddy the Pooka. "Three cheers for the duke and duchess."

And with the hurrahs of the crowd echoing in their ears, the royal party entered the town hall.

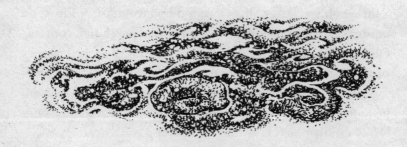

The Time Witches

8

Paddy the Pooka Sees a Strange Shadow

The crowd around the steps of the town hall began to disperse after the royal party had entered, but Paddy the Pooka lingered for a few moments. Something wasn't quite right.

As he had called out, "Hip, hip hooray," he had seen something out of the corner of his eye. It had moved like a shadow and vanished among the feet of the royal party as they entered the building.

Paddy felt an itch in his ears and a tingling in his front hooves. These were special signs to a pooka that something with evil intentions was close by. He decided to investigate.

Inside the town hall, the mayor had shown the royal guests to their sitting room and provided tea, served in Mrs. Mainbrace's best china. The king and queen now sat by a window with a view over the harbor. While the adults talked, Princess Galcia sat beside Abby as Spike whispered to her about how he had spent his vacation in Speller.

"What news of Wolfbane and his Night Witches, Sir Chadwick?" the king asked.

"I have little useful information, sir," replied Sir Chadwick as he munched on a sausage roll. "Their old headquarters on the Thames doesn't exist anymore. Mandini and I blew it up last month."

The king looked thoughtful. "We destroyed their Shark Boat port at Lantua. But I fear that will not be enough to put an end to them."

"There has been no sign of them anywhere on the world's oceans, sir," said Captain Starlight. "I have spoken to the whales. They have seen nothing."

"And Hilda's friends among the birds report no sightings of Wolfbane on land," said Mandini.

"What do you think, Sir Chadwick?" asked the king.

Sir Chadwick took a sip of tea before he answered. "We know Wolfbane is alive, sir, and as long as he is, he will strive to do evil. His vanity is so great he will certainly be plotting revenge for his defeat. We'll know no lasting peace until he is destroyed forever."

"What can you do, Sir Chadwick?" asked the queen. "He could strike anywhere at any time."

"We can only be vigilant, ma'am. The Light Witches may appear to be frivolous and vain, but they are brave and kind at heart, and they are all prepared for the worst Wolfbane can do."

The king nodded. Before answering, he looked out of the window at Speller and the sea beyond. "This really is an enchanting place," he said. "Has a history been written of the town?"

Abby, who had remained silent, listening to Galcia and Spike's whispered conversation, now stepped forward. "My mother and father are writing one at the moment, Your Grace."

The king looked at her with interest. "They are? Well I'll

look forward to reading it. How far have they got with their research?"

Abby smiled. "Well, there are papers all over the lighthouse where we live. The townsfolk have been very helpful with old records. Just this morning, my father showed me a diary that told how my ancestor Jack Elvin came to settle in Speller."

"Really," said the king, with growing enthusiasm. "So you know the exact date your ancestor settled here?"

"To the very hour," replied Abby.

With her attention directed at the king, she did not notice that something was moving in the shadows by the door. Nor did anyone else in the room. They were all watching the queen with sudden fascination as she struggled to stifle a yawn. It took a great deal of effort on her part, and some strange facial contortions, but she managed.

Sir Chadwick took this as a hint and said, "You must be tired after your voyage, ma'am. May I suggest we withdraw."

The queen smiled gratefully at his thoughtfulness. "I hope we'll have the pleasure of your company at dinner, Sir Chadwick. We will look forward to seeing Hilda Bluebell and the rest of our friends."

The men bowed formally and Abby opened the door. She was watching the queen struggling to suppress another yawn and didn't notice the shadowy form scuttle from the room ahead of her.

Sir Chadwick and Abby were the last to leave the king's quarters. As they followed the others across the lobby of the town hall, they heard a voice hiss, "Pssst, Chaddy, hang on a moment."

Sir Chadwick only just managed to suppress a groan.

Abby and Sir Chadwick spun around to see an enormous donkey filling most of the high-roofed hallway. The pooka had to bend his head low to avoid striking it on the decorated ceiling. "Just give me a minute," Paddy said. "I'm going to make a few minor adjustments."

There was a gentle popping sound as he shrank down to the size of a dog. "Too small," he muttered. The popping sound came again and he took on the normal dimensions of a donkey.

"Almost there," he said with a sigh. There were yet more popping sounds, and he stood before them in quite a new shape.

Paddy now had the body of a human being. He wore a green tweed suit, orange elastic-sided boots, and a bright yellow shirt with a large red handkerchief knotted around his throat. But his head remained that of a donkey.

"Good heavens!" exclaimed Sir Chadwick. You look just like Bottom in *A Midsummer Night's Dream*."

"That darlin' fella Shakespeare could sure write. But I think the character Bottom was a bit of a fool, meself."

"You're familiar with the play?" asked Sir Chadwick.

Paddy raised an eyebrow. "Haven't I played it on the stage of the Abbey Theater in Dublin?"

"You're an actor, Paddy?" said Abby, unable to disguise her surprise.

"A fellow Thespian, like Sir Chadwick — some of the time," nodded Paddy.

"Forgive me," said Sir Chadwick. "I should have realized."

"Sure, and there's no way of you knowing," said Paddy, "with meself done up like a donkey. When I tread the boards, I look like this." There was another popping sound and for a fleeting moment Paddy's features were transformed into a darkly handsome man with a classic profile. "My stage name is Patrick Oscar Fitzgerald."

"Of course," said Sir Chadwick, snapping his fingers. "I'm very familiar with your work, my dear fellow."

"Well, that's great, Chaddy, darlin'. But it wasn't what I wanted to talk to you about." He glanced around him and then drew closer to Abby and Sir Chadwick. "There's something peculiar going on around here."

Sir Chadwick looked puzzled. "The wedding, do you mean?" he asked.

Paddy shook his head. "No, something to do with Night Witches." He glanced over his shoulder again. "We pookas have the second sight, you know."

Sir Chadwick nodded. "So I've heard."

"Have you got any idea what the Night Witches are up to?" asked Abby.

Paddy shook his head. "Just a feeling. But I'm never wrong, so be on your guard."

"We will," replied Sir Chadwick and Abby, quickly looking about them. When they returned their gaze to where Paddy had been standing, the figure had vanished. Abby thought she could detect the faint aroma of peat smoke.

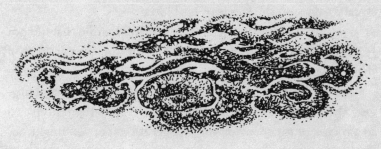

9

Sid Rollin Dines with the Night Witches

Wolfbane sat at the head of the dining table in the great hall of Darkwood Manor. He felt back in control for the first time since he'd escaped from the palace of Lantua. A large fire, consisting of a great heap of Darkwood Manor's priceless antique furniture and paintings, blazed in the hearth. Rancid-smelling candles lit the room, dripping their yellow wax on to the Oriental carpets.

Night Witches were crammed around the table, swilling wine from the bottles they had discovered in the cellar. They were all munching dreadful, smelly hamburgers, which they snatched from the heaped plates before them.

Next to Wolfbane sat Sid Rollin. He smiled uneasily at the behavior of the Night Witches and occasionally wiped his sweaty palms on the lapels of his blazer.

"So, Mr. Rollin," Wolfbane began, with a smile that did not reach his eyes. "You are responsible for the preparation of these culinary delights."

Sid Rollin nodded vigorously. "If you mean the hamburgers, Mr. Wolfbane, yes, that is indeed so. I have them prepared to a recipe of my own devising. A secret recipe, you might say.

I'm glad your colleagues find them appetizing. I always aim to please."

"And just what is in them?" asked Wolfbane, chewing savagely on his own selection.

Rollin avoided Wolfbane's eyes when he replied. "Oh, I'm afraid that's a trade secret, sir."

Wolfbane chuckled and looked along the table to where one of the Night Witches had just reached out for her third hamburger. "Elsie Cockroach, may I have your attention?"

The Night Witch looked in his direction with bloodshot eyes and, using the hem of her cloak to wipe a dribble of brown liquid from her whiskered chin, she answered, "Yes, Great One."

"You're something of a cook, Elsie," continued Wolfbane, holding up his hamburger. "Can you tell me the ingredients of these excellent concoctions?"

Elsie Cockroach paused for a moment and the sound of belching and gurgling came from the other Night Witches. She rolled her eyes up to the ceiling and took a nibble from the hamburger in her hand and chewed thoughtfully.

"Scrag end of cow's leg," she said slowly. "Pig's feet . . . quite a lot of rat . . . some mice, not too many, though . . . a sprinkling of bluebottles." She chewed again. "And old butcher's sawdust. . . . Quite delicious."

Wolfbane spoke to Rollin again. "You see, you are in the presence of gourmets. It was kind of you to deliver this order personally."

Sid Rollin gave a sickly smile and half rose from the table, as if to depart. "Think nothing of it. Well, if that's all, sir, I'll be going about my business."

Wolfbane gestured for him to sit down. "Nonsense," he said easily. "Have another glass of this excellent claret. The evening is far from over. Besides, I'll need you by and by."

Mr. Rollin sat down again and puffed unhappily on the cigar Wolfbane had presented to him. He bitterly regretted having agreed to deliver the hamburgers. He had never seen such an unspeakable collection of individuals in his life.

Rollin looked along the table at the row of black-cloaked figures. There were men and women, young and old. But one thing they had in common. They were all filthy dirty.

Blackened fingernails, grimy necks, greasy hair, and grubby clothes were the general rule. And, now the room was warming from the roaring fire, the smell was making him feel distinctly queasy. It was an unusual condition for Sid Rollin, whose stomach was accustomed to some foul situations.

Then he noticed another person joining the company. She sat opposite him on the other side of Mr. Wolfbane. To his surprise, she looked quite clean and he could not help staring at her.

"Is there something about my appearance that puzzles you, Mr. Rollin?" she asked with a gracious smile. Sid Rollin shook his head. "No, madam. I was just thinking how elegant you were. So nicely turned out, I mean."

"Why, thank you," she said with another smile. "One does one's best to keep up appearances. For instance, this dress is by Jean-Paul Gaultier. But the thing I'm proudest of is my designer dirt."

"Designer dirt?" Rollin repeated weakly.

She nodded. "You think I'm as clean as a new pin, don't you?"

"Yes," agreed Rollin.

The woman laughed lightly. "Watch this." She snapped her

The Time Witches

fingers and her appearance was transformed. Suddenly, she was as grubby as all the others seated around the table. The white collar of her dress was streaked with grime and there were food stains running down her front. Her hair hung in lank greasy tendrils, and her face and hands were ingrained with dirt.

She laughed at Rollin's startled expression and revealed a mouth full of crooked yellow teeth. Then she snapped her fingers again and returned to her previous pristine appearance. "Designer dirt," she said proudly. "Every Night Witch should have it in her makeup case."

Rollin shivered. "Night Witches, eh?" he said quickly. "Is that some kind of amateur theatrical company?"

Wolfbane, who had been listening to Rollin's conversation with his mother, suddenly snarled, "Amateur dramatics! Do you take us for a bunch of Light Witches? *They* are the strutting actors. What you see with us is the real thing."

Rollin was close to panic, his heart thudding alarmingly. "But there are no witches," he gasped desperately. "They're just a lot of hogwash for children."

"Really?" sneered Wolfbane. He summoned one of his cohorts. "Open the window. I feel Baal approaching."

The Night Witch did his bidding. After a moment, Rollin was confronted by a sight more terrifying than anything he had ever dreamed of in his worst nightmares.

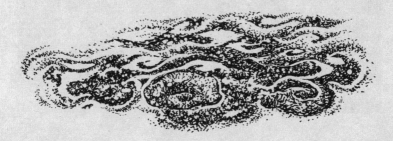

10

Raising the Spirit of Ma Hemlock

The dreadful creature that froze Sid Rollin to his chair was a massive black-and-yellow spider. It crouched in the flickering candlelight, framed by the open window. Its body was the size of a cat, but its hairy legs spread across the entire width of the windowsill. The spider paused for a moment before leaping onto the table in front of Wolfbane.

"Mr. Rollin," Wolfbane purred with satisfaction. "Let me introduce you to Baal, my familiar."

"Your familiar?" Rollin repeated faintly.

Wolfbane nodded. "It's a term used for the creatures we Night Witches have as pets and assistants. Legend has it that they are always black cats. As you see, that is not so."

"How did it get so big?" Rollin asked, curious despite his horror.

Wolfbane smiled and gestured with his cigar. "I owe that to my mother. She supplied me with the necessary potion, I merely boosted its performance with something of my own. Here, you see the result."

Sid Rollin recovered slightly. He began to rise slowly from his seat. Wolfbane gestured again with his cigar. "Baal," he commanded. "Secure him."

With startling speed, the gigantic spider spun a glistening cord from its body, looped it about Sid Rollin's shoulders, and bound him to his chair.

Wolfbane sat back in his seat with satisfaction. "Now, Baal, tell me what you have discovered about my enemies."

The spider drew close to its master and began to whisper in his ear.

"Wonderful," said Wolfbane after a time. "And you actually visited the lighthouse and saw the documents Abby Clover's parents have gathered?" The spider continued to whisper, and Wolfbane nodded in satisfaction.

"So, now I know, Jack Elvin is the key to it all," he exclaimed finally. "If I remove him from history, my problems will vanish like melted snow."

Wolfbane stood up. "Night Witches, I now possess all the information I need. Prepare torches. We'll consult Ma Hemlock about the next part of my plan."

The Night Witches began to break up more furniture and wrap oily rags about the lengths of wood.

"What about me, Mr. Wolfbane?" Rollin squeaked.

"Oh, yes," Wolfbane said genially. "Well, you see, Mr. Rollin, I now have to perform a very powerful spell." He produced a folded document from the inside pocket of his coat and opened it. "Yes," he said after a moment's study. "It states quite clearly that this spell requires the blood of a butcher."

Sid Rollin went deathly pale in the candlelight. "But I'm not just a butcher, Mr. Wolfbane. I'm a prominent businessman in several fields of endeavor."

Wolfbane waggled a finger. "Now, now, Mr. Rollin, don't seek to escape your fate on a technicality. Just remember that your blood will be used to write a new and glorious chapter in the history of the Night Witches."

He looked about him for a moment. "But what will we carry it in?" he said. His gaze fell on his familiar. "Ah, yes, I think Baal can do that." Wolfbane addressed the spider. "Baal, bring me all of Mr. Rollin's blood."

The Night Witches watched with admiration as the giant spider leaped onto Sid Rollin's chest and attached its mouth to his main artery. There was a gurgling sound, and Sid Rollin began to deflate like a punctured balloon. Baal's body swelled even larger. Eventually, Baal withdrew and the awful, sagging bag of skin and bones that had been Sid Rollin collapsed in a jumbled heap on the chair.

"To Ma Hemlock's grave," Wolfbane shouted.

Lighting their torches from the fire, the Night Witches flanked Wolfbane as he led them through the grounds of the manor house. Baal waddled behind them.

The procession passed the ornamental lake and followed

Wolfbane to the clearing in the wood. He instructed the Night Witches to stand in a circle around the gnarled and twisted tree with the strange, fleshy leaves.

"Do you have the instructions with you, Mother?" Wolfbane asked.

Lucia Cheeseman stepped forward. She held a book open and ran her finger down the page. "Bring that torch closer," she instructed one of the Night Witches. She held out the open page to show Wolfbane. "The ground at the foot of the Witch Tree must be soaked with butcher's blood," she said.

Wolfbane paused briefly before asking his mother, "Do you think that means the blood of a butcher or blood gathered from a butcher shop?"

Lucia shrugged. "We'll soon know if it doesn't work," she replied impatiently. "Let's get on with it."

Wolfbane nodded, then gestured to Baal. The creature scuttled forward and squirted Sid Rollin's blood in a long stream around the roots of the Witch Tree.

"What now?" Wolfbane asked.

"Recite this," said his mother.

Wolfbane peered at the page and chanted:

"Blood of a butcher, heart of a crow,
Defy Mother Nature and send us black snow.
We who do evil beg for this sign,
Grant us this wish and our souls remain thine."

Wolfbane looked at the book again. "Do we have the heart of a crow?" he asked. As he spoke there was a fluttering of wings and Caspar, Lucia's raven, suddenly perched on her shoulder. The bird held something grisly in his beak.

"Go and put that at the foot of the tree, there's a good boy," Lucia whispered, and the raven flew to do her bidding.

Wolfbane felt something wet on his cheeks. He held out his hand and saw that it was spotted with black snowflakes.

"Now the last verse," Lucia prompted softly. Wolfbane looked down to the book and recited:

"Spirit in the nether regions,
We call on you for special reasons,
Leave the silence of the earth,
Return to us, who know thy worth,
Cast aside the sleep of time,
From the grave we bid you climb,
Defy the bounds of death's dark strife,
Assume the shape you had in life."

Although the black snow continued to fall, the sky was clear apart from a single dark cloud that half covered the full moon. There was absolute silence for a time, then came a deep rumbling sound in the distance, as though a thousand galloping horses were thundering toward them.

The sky filled with dark storm clouds and lightning crashed all around. A great howling wind whipped the flames of the Night Witches' torches, so they flared even brighter in the darkness. Lucia's raven hopped inside her cloak to shelter from a sudden squall of lashing rain.

"Look!" shouted Wolfbane.

The Night Witches followed his pointing finger to gaze at the twisted tree. It glowed with an unearthly green light, and a new sound began as the wind dropped to an eerie moan. The noise was like the insistent throbbing of a monstrous heart.

With each menacing beat, the tree quivered like a living thing. Slowly, its shape started to alter. The trunk contorted to take on the appearance of a woman's huddled body. Two of the lower branches reached out like arms drawing the power of the storm toward itself.

The throbbing beat ceased, and a low scream began. Softly, at first, then with such dreadful intensity that even Wolfbane was forced to hold his hands to his ears. The shattering scream died away as the tree straightened to complete its nightmarish metamorphosis.

A truly terrible figure stood before them.

Wolfbane recognized the danger of calling up this hideous creature, invested as she was with all of the powers of evil. Although her flesh, where it showed through the tattered remains of a shroud, was crinkled with age, sinewy muscles rippled as she stretched each arm in turn.

Clawlike hands reached up and parted the long, straggling dirty-white hair that hung like a matted veil over her features. A face even more vile than his own stared back at Wolfbane.

Skin as dry as parchment covered the bones of her skull, and a long sharp nose dipped to almost meet her pointed chin. The apparition's eyes glittered a venomous green. A deep grating sound started in her throat, gradually giving way to a cackle of exaltation. Her yellow teeth were jagged like a shark's.

"Who calls me?" the figure moaned.

Wolfbane stepped forward. "I do. Wolfbane, Grand Master of the Night Witches."

"Come closer, Wolfbane," the figure instructed, beckoning him with a skeletal hand. "What do you want, Grand Master of the Night Witches? Why have you called me from the grave?"

"I want to know your secret of time travel," Wolfbane answered.

"The Wizards banned time travel without their permission," the specter moaned.

"I know that, Ma Hemlock," Wolfbane replied.

"Don't call me *that*," the apparition snapped angrily. "I hate the name Ma. Call me Matilda."

"I do beg your pardon, Matilda," Wolfbane hastened to say. Then, smoothly regaining his composure, he continued, "Can you grant me the wish I ask?"

"Why do you want to travel in time?" she asked slyly.

"Vengeance," Wolfbane replied, his voice thin with hatred.

"You don't want to do *good*, do you?"

"Only for myself."

Ma Hemlock nodded contentedly. "So, if I grant you this wish, you will cause someone pain and grief?"

"Many people, yes."

"Splendid," said the gaunt figure before him. "Vengeance, selfishness, and cruelty. Motives after my own heart. I shall grant your wish."

The storm ended as abruptly as it had begun. Ma Hemlock pointed at the moon, which was peeping from behind the clouds. "This will be your means of traveling through time."

"The moon?" asked Wolfbane, puzzled.

"Wait," said the apparition of Ma Hemlock.

Wolfbane looked into the sky and gradually made out a black dot against the silver surface of the moon. It seemed to be growing, and a strange moaning began. The dot grew bigger and bigger until Wolfbane could make out a frightening shape.

Four horse skeletons with plumes attached to their skulls

drew an open black carriage through the sky toward the Night Witches.

As it grew closer, Wolfbane could see a cloaked coachman was driving the team. But he was not a living creature. Beneath a black top hat grimaced a skull. Skeletal hands held the reins and clasped a long whip.

The nightmarish team and carriage descended to the clearing and drew up before Ma Hemlock. "This is my private coachman," she said. "He can drive you through time."

"How will I summon him?" Wolfbane asked, his yellow eyes glittering in anticipation.

"Look in the palm of your left hand," Ma Hemlock instructed.

Wolfbane saw a strange design burned into his skin. "It's a pentangle," he said. "But I don't recognize the symbols."

Ma Hemlock chuckled. "Six thousand years before your time, Wolfbane. They're from ancient Sumeria. Believe me, they work. Draw that and the coach will come."

"What is that space for, beneath the dog with the fish's head?" asked Wolfbane, pointing to his hand.

"That's where you write the date to which you wish to travel. You must be precise. Give the exact time — to the second."

"Thank you, Matilda," Wolfbane said, his face almost transformed with elation. "Is there anything I can do for you?"

Ma Hemlock shook her wild hair and climbed into the coach.

"No, thank you, Wolfbane," she replied, leaning back into the black velvet upholstery. "I always say, *badness is its own reward.*"

Wolfbane looked about him in triumph, but Ma Hemlock held up a finger. "A warning. Be careful, Wolfbane. Something dangerous lies in wait for you."

"What?"

"The first female among Light Witches could bring great grief to you. That is my warning."

Wolfbane looked puzzled. "The first female among Light Witches," he repeated. "Who is that?" he called out, but Ma Hemlock had muttered her instructions to the coachman, and the dreadful carriage with its ghostly horses was already galloping across the sky.

Wolfbane watched her depart, and repeated, "*The first female among Light Witches.* What the devil can that mean?" Then he slapped his forehead. "Chadwick Street is marrying that *oh-so-sweet* little actress, Hilda Bluebell. That will make *her* the first female among Light Witches. She must be the danger."

Wolfbane strode toward the manor house with a determined expression. "Well, we'll soon see about that."

11

The Mystery of the Old Photograph Album

T he clocks in Speller were chiming eight on the morning of the wedding. Mr. Mainbrace was in the kitchen of their apartment in the attic of the town hall, about to enjoy his breakfast of two lightly boiled eggs. The mayor had a hearty appetite because he had been up at dawn arranging the weather for the day.

Starting with a good shower of rain to freshen up the town, he had decided on a bright cool morning with a scattering of clouds. Not too warm, because he knew from experience that there was always a good deal of rushing about on these occasions, and he didn't want anyone to get too hot and bothered.

Mrs. Mainbrace had also risen early because she was in charge of the wedding feast. After the ceremony, all of the townsfolk and guests were to assemble in the great tent where the banquet would be served.

They were going to have fresh seafood cocktails to start, followed by roasted duckling in cherry sauce, an apple crumble with clotted cream, and a selection of Speller cheeses.

Mrs. Mainbrace was still worried that the meal would be

too heavy, but Mr. Mainbrace reassured her that it was just what the bride and groom wanted.

"Well, I think it's just Sir Chadwick who wants roasted duckling," grumbled Mrs. Mainbrace. "I'm sure Hilda would prefer a selection of delicious salads on such a warm summer's day."

"How are the duke and duchess and Princess Galcia?" Mr. Mainbrace asked, changing the subject.

"They slept well," his wife informed him. "I've just taken them breakfast in their rooms. Now I'm going to the baker's to check on the fresh rolls for the wedding feast."

Mr. Mainbrace looked from his window toward the harbor. "The fishing boat is coming in. Let's hope they had a good catch for the seafood cocktails."

In the harbor, Captain Starlight stood on the deck of the *Ishmael* and watched the fishing boat unload the catch. Benbow circled above the boat until one of the Sea Witches threw him a plump mackerel for his breakfast.

Benbow was quite capable of catching his own fish, but he did like to be waited on from time to time.

"Morning, Captain."

Starlight looked up to see the Great Mandini and Sir Chadwick standing on the jetty.

"Permission to come aboard?" requested Mandini.

"I've just made some fresh coffee," replied Starlight with a grin. "Would you care for a cup?"

"I'm sure the groom would," said Mandini. "He's got a stomachache. Too many pints of Speller Special Brew last night, I wouldn't wonder."

"Nonsense," said Sir Chadwick gruffly. "But I would like a cup of coffee."

Captain Starlight went below and returned from the galley with two steaming mugs.

Sir Chadwick was about to drink from his when he suddenly put down the mug. "Oh, dear," he said anxiously. "I forgot the wedding rings. Oh, dear. This is a disaster."

Captain Starlight winked at Mandini and produced two bands of gold from the pocket of his pea jacket. "I remembered," he said.

"Well done, Adam," Sir Chadwick said faintly. "Where would I be without you?"

"They are splendid," said Mandini, examining the rings. "Where did you get them, Adam?"

Captain Starlight sipped his own coffee as he glanced out to sea. "From the wreck of a Spanish treasure galleon I found off Key Largo. They were made for a prince of Spain and his bride."

Just then, the sound of children singing came from the church.

"Reverend Cannon is having a final rehearsal," said Starlight. "Not long now."

"I suppose we'd better bathe and change into our dress clothes," said Mandini.

Starlight nodded. "I'll come to the Speller Tavern at about nine-thirty so we can walk to the church together." He glanced up at Benbow who, with long lazy strokes of his wings, rose from the jetty and flew toward the lighthouse.

Abby stood in her bedroom and looked at herself in the full-length mirror on the stone wall. Her mother was standing behind her. "You look lovely, darling," she said reassuringly. Abby was more dubious. When she bothered to look at herself in a mirror, she was used to seeing herself in a fisherman's smock.

Abby hardly recognized her own reflection. She wore a long cream-colored dress with short puff sleeves and an old-fashioned bonnet and white gloves. She carried a small basket full of wildflowers. "How do I sit down with this big bow at the back?" she asked gloomily.

"Very carefully," replied her mother with an affectionate laugh.

Her father appeared in the doorway. "Help me with the back stud on this collar, Madge," he said, peering into the room. "Hello," he added, surprised. "Who is this little girl? Has anyone seen my daughter, Abby? She always dresses like a fisherman."

"Very funny, Dad," said Abby. "I feel like a doll."

"So do I," said Spike, who had replaced Mr. Clover in the doorway. He was wearing a soldier's white uniform with gold braid. A sword hung at his side.

"At least you've got a sword," Abby said enviously. "Can you do anything with it?"

Spike shook his head. "It's only a ceremonial sword. I suppose I could knight someone with it, but it's no good for cutting things."

"Now, you two go and make yourselves useful," Mrs. Clover said.

"What should we do?" asked Abby.

"The papers on the history of Speller are scattered all over the study. Put them in a neat pile next to the desk. And try not to get dust on your clothes."

"How can we do that?" grumbled Spike as they made their way to the study. "I just have to stand still and I get dusty."

"I can make sure we stay clean," said Abby.

"How?"

"It's one of the first things I was taught in Light Witchcraft lessons," said Abby. "You see, Light Witches like to be clean. That's one of the big differences between Night Witches and us. They prefer to be dirty and smell awful."

She faced Spike and chanted.

"Make us good.
Make us kind,
Make us clean
In body and mind."

"Is that all?" said Spike, unimpressed. "No bangs or puffs of smoke? Are you sure it worked?"

"Try and get dirty," Abby said.

"That's easy for me," Spike said a trifle gloomily.

Suddenly, Benbow appeared on the windowsill and Spike spoke to him. "Do me a favor, Benbow. Will you bring me something to make my hands dirty?"

The bird flew away and moments later returned with a thick stick of wood coated in black oil that he had found floating in the bay.

"Watch," Spike said, seizing the stick in his hands before throwing it from the open window. He looked at his hands and to his astonishment saw they were both quite clean.

"Amazing," he exclaimed. "Now, that's what I call a very useful spell."

"Come on," said Abby. "Let's get all these papers tidy."

"What is all this stuff?" asked Spike as Abby piled his arms high.

"Documents my parents collected from the people of Speller about the history of the town," Abby answered. She

The Time Witches

held up the little red diary from which her father had read the passage about Josiah Bowsprit first meeting Jack Elvin.

"Is there anything interesting?" asked Spike.

"Here's an album of photographs," replied Abby, reading the name on the binding. "Mary Bowsprit, she was my ancestor. I don't think anyone has looked at them yet."

"Show me," said Spike, and Abby passed him the heavy book.

"Speller hasn't changed much," said Spike as he leafed through the pages. Then he stopped. "Hey, look at this, Abby. Here's something very odd." Abby looked over his shoulder at the sepia-colored picture. It showed the vacation resort of Torgate at a time when the pier was still standing. Crowds of tourists thronged the promenade, the women in long dresses and big hats and the men wearing striped blazers and straw boaters.

Tied up to the end of the pier was the Atlantis Boat!

The Mystery of the Old Photograph Album

There could be no doubt. Abby recognized her sleek lines immediately. Three people stood on the deck.

Abby took a big magnifying glass from the desk and looked closer. The figures were Captain Starlight, the Great Mandini, and Spike. The children looked at each other in astonishment but before they could speak, Abby's mother called out, "Abby, Spike, hurry, it's time to take your places in the bridal procession."

12

Wolfbane Strikes Out

Abby and Spike ran down the spiral staircase and joined the others who were part of the bridal procession. Abby's father, Harry, looked very grand in his frock coat and top hat. He was going to give the bride away, so he and Hilda took the lead.

Next came Abby and Spike, carrying the bride's train. Then Abby's mother and her mom's sister, Aunt Lucy, dressed as matrons of honor. Uncle Ben was already at the church with the Speller Town Band.

"Oh, dear," said Lucy to her sister. "Walking along the path with our long dresses trailing will make them awfully dusty."

"Don't worry," Abby said, and she repeated her spell to ward off dirt.

Spike grinned. "Have you got a spell that wards off boredom as well? They say the wedding ceremony goes on and on and only the grown-ups have a good time."

"Nonsense, Spike," Abby replied loftily, as she took up the bride's train. "It'll be fun, won't it, Hilda?"

Two doves flew close to Hilda and a chorus of thrushes and blackbirds started to sing. "I'm not bored," she answered. "But I do feel very nervous."

Abby had intended to mention the photograph of the Atlantis Boat, but before she could speak her father called out. "All ready? Off we go."

As the procession walked along the cliff path, a bitter wind began to blow from the direction of Darkwood Forest. Gentle gusts at first, it grew stronger and colder with each step they took.

"I think Mr. Mainbrace has overdone the breeze a bit," Harry Clover said loudly as he held on to his top hat in the ever-strengthening wind.

"Keep a good grip on the train, children," Abby's mother called out anxiously.

Abby looked in the direction of Darkwood Forest and saw storm clouds rolling toward them. There was a strange light in the sky. High above, Benbow circled. He seemed to be calling out a warning.

A dark shape was growing in the sky. The wind was so strong now they could hardly stand. The air filled with a dreadful howling — it sounded like a thousand people shrieking in agony.

The menacing shape in the sky took on a recognizable form. Abby shouted out a warning, but it was too late. Ma Hemlock's spectral carriage was upon them.

Abby saw Wolfbane, savage exaltation on his face, reach down and snatch Hilda into the carriage. Abby's father tried to seize the train of Hilda's wedding dress, but the skeletal horses reared up and knocked him to the ground.

The spectral coachman whipped the horses and the carriage rose, bearing Wolfbane and the struggling Hilda into the storm-torn sky.

Abby didn't pause to think. Throwing off her cumbersome bridesmaid dress and bonnet, she called out to Benbow. He swooped down to hover above her. She grabbed hold of his legs and shouted, "Follow the coach, Benbow!" As they rose into the air, she saw Spike running along the cliff-top path toward the town, where the wedding party waited.

Benbow flew faster than Abby had ever known before. The wind in her face was so strong she could hardly whistle the tune that caused her to disappear, but she just managed to do so. Soon they were crossing Darkwood Forest. Below them she could see the railway line and the road to Torgate on each side of the great wood.

The coach was still ahead but was about to land. Abby and Benbow followed.

The empty carriage was standing in the gravel drive in front of Darkwood Manor. Night Witches were everywhere, but there was no sign of Wolfbane and Hilda.

Abby whispered to Benbow to take them up to the roof where she could look down on the empty carriage.

The Night Witches were making some sort of preparation with bags of powder that Abby realized was Black Dust. They were sprinkling it to make a great star shape around the carriage.

Abby recognized it as a pentangle. When it was completed, the Night Witches began to form strange symbols with the Black Dust. Finally, they wrote a time and date. Abby made a mental note of it.

Suddenly, Wolfbane appeared carrying Hilda in his arms, followed by an elegantly dressed woman. Hilda was obviously in a deep sleep and no longer wore her bridal gown. Instead, she was dressed in the long, blue velvet costume of a Victorian lady.

Wolfbane took his place in the carriage and pointed at the remaining seats. "Mother, take your place opposite," he ordered. "The rest of you Night Witches return to your hiding places until I summon you again."

Lucia Cheeseman clambered aboard the carriage as the rest of the Night Witches rose like a flock of giant black bats and scattered to the four points of the compass.

Wolfbane shouted, "In the name of Ma Hemlock, I order you to go back in time!"

The howling began again, and Abby ducked down behind the parapet as the carriage rose in the air and vanished into the storm clouds. Gradually, the wind died away and a soft rain began to fall.

Abby was about to return to Speller to get help when she heard faint cries coming from below.

Benbow flew her to the ground and, following the sound through the open door of the manor house, she found her way to the cellar and the iron cage where Lord Darkwood, Jorrocks the butler, and the taxi driver were held captive. Fortunately, the key to their cage hung on a hook by the door.

The prisoners stumbled out in a dazed state, and Abby helped them back to the great hall. In her rush to return to Speller, she didn't notice the grisly bag of skin and bones that had once been Sid Rollin.

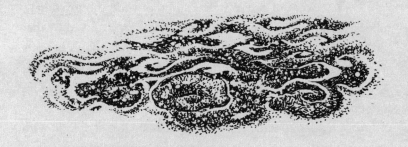

13

Another Message from Ma Hemlock

When Benbow landed her in the town square, Abby found the whole town in a state of shock. Clusters of Sea Witches stood outside the town hall, talking anxiously in low voices. Mrs. Mainbrace told Abby that Sir Chadwick, Captain Starlight, Mandini, and Abby's parents were gathered in the rooms of the king and queen of Lantua.

When she entered, she found Spike with them. He was no longer dressed in uniform.

Abby had expected to find Sir Chadwick stricken with grief, but instead he was in a grimly determined mood.

"We must pursue them," the king said angrily. "Sir Chadwick, the resources of my entire kingdom are at your disposal. As much Ice Dust as you need, and all the jewels in my treasury."

"Thank you, Your Majesty," Sir Chadwick replied. "But the first thing we need is more information. We must listen to Abby before we decide our course of action." He put a hand on her shoulder. "Tell us exactly what happened, child. Leave nothing out."

Abby described what she had heard and seen at Darkwood Manor. When she had finished, Sir Chadwick said, "Wolfbane's exact words were: *In the name of Ma Hemlock, I order you to go back in time?*"

Abby nodded.

"Ma Hemlock, Ma Hemlock," he repeated. "Who the devil is Ma Hemlock?"

"She must have some connection with Darkwood Manor," said Abby. "And she must be very powerful if Wolfbane can travel back into the past merely by invoking her name."

"How do you know that, child?" asked the king.

"From my witch lessons, sir."

"Abby is right. Evil has many strange properties, Your Majesty," Sir Chadwick explained. "But it loses power the farther away it is from its place of origin. Believe me, Darkwood Manor is the key to these events."

"Perhaps Lord Darkwood knows who Ma Hemlock is," Abby suggested.

Sir Chadwick nodded. "That may be so. We must go to Darkwood Manor and question him."

"How will we get there?" asked Mandini.

"The Atlantis Boat," Sir Chadwick replied.

"Where is it now?" asked Captain Starlight.

"Somewhere in the bay," Spike informed them. "I saw it yesterday when I was swimming with the dolphins."

"And whom will you take on this vital expedition?" the king asked.

Sir Chadwick looked about him and smiled for the first time. "Who else but the crew who last defeated the Night Witches?"

A few minutes later, Sir Chadwick led his party down to the harbor. Abby stood on the jetty and gave a long piercing whistle.

Immediately, the Atlantis Boat bobbed to the surface.

Every time Abby saw the sleek little craft, its beauty gave her a tingle of pleasure. In some ways, it reminded her of an elegant creature from the sea. The silvery metal of the hull appeared to be fashioned from the scales of a great fish, and the cabin was shaped rather like the shell of a giant turtle.

Abby and Spike waved good-bye to their parents and joined Starlight, Mandini, and Sir Chadwick in the snug little cabin. There were deep velvety seats fitted with safety belts, a small galley, and a chart table with a great crystal ball set in the center.

Captain Starlight took the controls and, as soon as they were out of the harbor, opened up the throttle. The little craft hurtled along the coast toward Torgate. The journey took less than three minutes.

Captain Starlight slowed the Atlantis Boat and steered her toward a heap of pebbles on the rock-strewn beach. Gently, he thrust the prow deep into the heap so they could all step off it onto dry land.

A lone figure stood on the beach, watching them as they disembarked. Abby recognized him as the young man Wolfbane had imprisoned at Darkwood Manor.

"Aren't you driving your taxi anymore?" she asked him.

He shook his head. "I can't forget what happened to me, miss," he said in a quivering voice. "It was horrible in that dungeon."

"What are you doing now?" asked Mandini.

"Thought I'd take up beachcombing," he replied, glancing around at the rock-strewn beach. "But there isn't much to salvage around here."

Mandini smiled and held up his hands in front of the youth's face. "Look into the eyes of the Great Mandini," he said, waving his hands gently. "You will forget all that happened to you at Darkwood Manor. When I snap my fingers, it will be as if it never took place. Do you understand?"

The taxi driver nodded. Mandini snapped his fingers and the youth looked at them keenly. He gazed around the beach in a bewildered fashion and asked, "What am I doing down here?"

"We called you," Mandini said smoothly. "We want you to take us to Darkwood Manor."

"My cab's up there on the promenade," the youth said, suddenly cheerful. "It won't take but a few seconds to get there."

They climbed some steps from the beach. Just before they climbed into the battered taxi, Abby noticed a bronze plaque set in the pavement. It read:

IN MEMORY OF THE PEOPLE WHO LOST THEIR LIVES
IN THE GREAT PIER DISASTER OF JUNE 15, 1894

As they pulled away, Mandini looked along the dreary length of the windswept promenade and said, "What a miserable little town. I'm glad I have never had to perform here."

"It wasn't always like this," said the taxi driver. "My grandmother said her grandmother used to have a great time in Torgate."

"Things change," said Sir Chadwick. "Not always for the better."

Soon the taxi was turning into the drive of Darkwood Manor.

"This is a grim-looking place," said Spike.

Captain Starlight rolled up his window after sniffing the air. "Night Witches," he muttered, so the youth driving could not hear. "I can always smell them."

When they had parked outside the manor house, Sir Chadwick rang the bell and a voice from inside shouted, "Go away!"

"That's Jorrocks, the butler," said Abby.

Sir Chadwick glanced over his shoulder to make sure the taxi driver wasn't watching, then tapped on the massive iron-door handle with the wand he had concealed up his sleeve. The door swung open and they entered.

In the Great Hall, they found Lord Darkwood slumped in front of a smoldering fire. In one of the few remaining chairs opposite was a ghastly sight — the dried-out remains of Sid Rollin. Sir Chadwick quickly examined the skin and bones inside the blazer and flannel trousers. "Night Witch work," he said grimly.

"Get me two buckets of water. And be as quick as you can," Sir Chadwick ordered the butler who was hovering behind them.

"I beg your pardon," he answered haughtily.

Mandini gestured quickly with his hands in front of Jorrocks's face, and the butler turned and walked toward the pantry. He returned almost immediately with the water. Mandini snapped his fingers again and ordered the butler to return to the kitchen and stay there.

Sir Chadwick stirred both buckets of water vigorously with his wand, then slowly poured them over the body of Rollin. Almost at once, Rollin began to swell back to his normal size.

Rollin, restored to his usual plumpness, blinked a few times, and opened his eyes wide.

"Oh," he said weakly, ignoring everyone but Lord Darkwood. "I must have dozed off. I had a horrible dream, my lord." He got up shakily and shuffled toward the door. "Must be getting home now, the wife will be wondering what happened to me."

Sir Chadwick looked at Lord Darkwood, who continued to stare ahead, seemingly oblivious to his surroundings. "Can you do anything with him, Mandini?" he asked.

"I think so," the magician replied. He began to wave his hands in front of Lord Darkwood's face. After a few moments, Darkwood began to follow them with his eyes.

"Got him!" said Mandini.

"Ask him who Ma Hemlock is," said Sir Chadwick.

Mandini did so and Lord Darkwood began to speak softly. When he was finished, Mandini said, "You will sleep for three hours and, when you awake, you will have forgotten everything about Wolfbane's visit. You will think all your missing furniture was destroyed in a fire."

Lord Darkwood closed his eyes and after a moment began to snore gently.

Sir Chadwick addressed the others.

"Wolfbane has been playing a dangerous game. He has broken the Wizards' Treaty by calling up the dead and traveling in time without official permission."

"What is the Wizards' Treaty?" asked Abby.

"I'll explain later," Sir Chadwick replied. "Meanwhile, we must have a talk with this Ma Hemlock."

"There might still be a trace of her spirit about the house," said Mandini.

"What do you suggest?" Sir Chadwick asked him.

Mandini thought for a moment. "It would take some time to raise her entire specter," he said. "But perhaps we can get her spirit to take possession of Lord Darkwood."

Sir Chadwick nodded. "It might work. At least it's worth a try." He looked down on Lord Darkwood, who continued to slumber peacefully.

Sir Chadwick made several elaborate gestures in the air with his wand and said, "We call on the spirit of Ma Hemlock. Are you still here?"

Sir Chadwick repeated the process several times, but Lord Darkwood didn't stir.

Suddenly, Abby felt a strange sensation, as if something inside were telling her to try her hand. "Let me try, Sir Chadwick," she said quietly.

Mandini was about to object when Sir Chadwick held up a hand. "Give her a chance," he said.

Ignoring Lord Darkwood, Abby turned to Spike. "Close your eyes and imagine you're under the sea," she said. "There's nothing around you but clear water."

Abby didn't say anything else. Instead, she closed her own eyes and concentrated as hard as she could, calling out with her mind for Ma Hemlock to speak through Spike.

"Nothing is happening," whispered Mandini.

Sir Chadwick held up his hand again.

Suddenly, Spike said, "Who calls on me?" The voice was that of an old woman.

"I do," said Abby. "With all the power of the Light Witches."

"What do you want?" said Ma Hemlock's spirit voice.

"Tell us what you told Wolfbane," said Abby sternly.

"Let me sleep, I'm tired," the old voice said petulantly.

"I command you, Ma Hemlock. Repeat your words."

The old woman's voice spoke again. "I said, the first female of the Light Witches will bring danger to Wolfbane when he goes into the past," the voice said. "Now let me rest."

Abby then spoke. "Wake up, Spike," she said.

Spike opened his eyes. "That was strange," he said. "I could hear that old woman talking in my head. When did you learn to perform that spell, Abby?"

"She has never been taught it," said Sir Chadwick, thoughtfully. "You can be a very surprising girl, Abby."

"Who is the first female among Light Witches?" asked Mandini.

"The old crone must have meant Hilda," said Captain Starlight. He stared at Sir Chadwick. "She will be the first female among the Light Witches when she marries you. That must be why Wolfbane has kidnapped her. I think he's going to kill her."

Mandini shook his head. "It's not just Hilda, Chadwick. I'm sure he wants his revenge on you, too, on all of us, in fact. For some reason Wolfbane wants to lure you into the past."

"I know," said Sir Chadwick. "But I have to follow her there, I can't just abandon Hilda."

"What can you do?" asked Abby.

"I must ask for an appointment with the Ministry of Time, immediately."

"This is a very dangerous business," Captain Starlight warned. "Wolfbane knows you will play the game according to the Wizards' rules, Chadwick. But he has no scruples about playing dirty. The past is a dangerous place."

"Nonetheless, it must be done," said Chadwick, walking to a desk that stood against the wall. He took a sheet of writing paper and scribbled a note with a gold fountain pen.

Folding the note twice and tapping it with his wand, he returned to the fireplace and threw it on the smoldering fire.

Abby and Spike watched in wonder as the paper burst into flames. After a moment, a fresh sheet of folded paper appeared in the fire. Sir Chadwick snatched it from the flames and read the message it contained.

"I have an appointment at the Ministry of Time, ten o'clock tomorrow morning." He paused, puzzled, then added, "They have instructed me to bring Abby."

"How do they know about me?" asked Abby, surprised.

Mandini shrugged his shoulders. "No one knows for sure what the Wizards know," he answered in a hushed voice.

Captain Starlight stood up briskly. "Well, there's nothing for us to do but return to Speller and have a good night's rest. You'll need all your wits about you at the Ministry of Time tomorrow."

As if to give emphasis to Starlight's words, Lord Darkwood gave an especially loud snore and settled deeper into his chair before the fire.

14

A Call from the Ministry of Coincidence

In the taxi on the return journey to the seafront at Torgate, Sir Chadwick told Abby and Spike all about the power of the Wizards.

Mandini had hypnotized the driver again, so he believed he was listening to Sir Chadwick talk about the history of blizzards.

"The problem of time travel all began hundreds and hundreds of years ago," Sir Chadwick began. "A war had been raging between the Night Witches and the Light Witches for as long as anyone could remember. Human beings weren't much bothered by the conflict, apart from occasional difficulties, like Black Death or the invention of gunpowder."

"They were caused by the Witch Wars?" interrupted Spike.

Sir Chadwick nodded. "Why do you think it was called *Black* Death? And the old-fashioned term for gunpowder was *black* powder. All the same, things were jogging along as usual, until a group of Night Witches broke into the Great Pyramid and found one of the secrets of time travel."

"*One* of the secrets?" said Abby.

"Oh, yes," said Sir Chadwick. "There are many ways to travel in time. You saw the method Wolfbane used to kidnap Hilda. It isn't the only one. But to continue. The Night Witches began to alter history, and the Wizards kept having to put things back as they should be.

"Then the Light Witches discovered ways to time travel. There would have been the most awful chaos, so the Wizards called a great treaty between the Night Witches and Light Witches. Both sides agreed to ban time travel, unless they were given a special permit by the Wizards at the Ministry of Time."

"Why are the Wizards so powerful?" asked Spike.

Sir Chadwick looked at him. "An interesting question, Spike. Legend has it that the Wizards aren't from this planet at all. But there are arguments about that. All we know is there have always been Wizards, even before Witches. It is said that the Wizards actually invented magic.

"They used to advise kings, but as kings gradually lost their influence, the Wizards broke away and set up their own great ministries of power."

"So they don't just run the Ministry of Time?" Abby asked.

"Oh, no, there's the Ministry of Regrets, the Ministry of Coincidence, the Ministry of Imagination, and the Ministry of Dreams. The Wizards are also the governing body of Merlin College, Oxford, although the day-to-day business of the college is conducted by Light Witch dons."

"Wizards must be very great people," said Abby.

"Hmmm," Sir Chadwick replied mysteriously. "You'll see tomorrow."

When they arrived back at the beach, Sir Chadwick paid the taxi driver and he roared away in a haze of exhaust fumes. On board the Atlantis Boat, Captain Starlight took the controls and set course for Speller. As they rounded the bay, he said, "Something very strange has happened."

They were looking at a bare cliff face. Speller had vanished!

Abby felt a wave of fear and turned quickly to Spike. "Our families," she said. "Where have they gone?"

Sir Chadwick held up a hand. "It may not be as bad as it seems," he said quickly. "Captain Starlight, take us closer to the shore, if you please." Then he held a hand out to Mandini. "Do you have your illusionist's spectacles with you?"

"Of course," replied Mandini, producing with a flourish a pair of sparkling silver-framed glasses.

Sir Chadwick donned them and said, "Just as I thought." They were close to the shore now, and Abby could make out a sign attached to a stake driven into the sand where the harbor wall had stood. It read:

THE TOWN OF SPELLER
IS NOW UNDER THE
JURISDICTION OF THE
MINISTRY OF COINCIDENCE

Abby read the sign aloud, then asked, "What does that mean?"

"Look through these," said Sir Chadwick, handing the spectacles to a worried Abby. She put them on and suddenly the town and its people reappeared. But there was no color or movement anywhere. The citizens were frozen in their everyday attitudes, as if they were part of a gigantic black-and-white photograph.

But then something moved. It was Benbow, flying toward them. He landed on the boat with a squawk of pleasure.

Captain Starlight chuckled. "No Wizard is going to tell you what to do, eh, old fellow?"

Benbow nodded in agreement.

"Why isn't Benbow frozen in time along with everyone else?" asked Abby.

Captain Starlight patted the great bird. "Wizards have no power over spirit animals," he said. "They come and go as they please. Even in *time* when it suits them."

"That's right," said Mandini. "Wizards can't control pookas, either — or Night Witch familiars, come to that."

"But what's happened to the townsfolk?" asked Spike when he had donned Mandini's spectacles.

"The Wizards are tying everything up with red tape," said Sir Chadwick grimly.

"But I thought we were dealing with the Ministry of Time, not the Ministry of Coincidence," said Abby.

"Nothing is ever simple when you're dealing with the Wizards," he answered. "They're always getting their wires crossed. You should hear the dons go on about how they interfere at Merlin College. No student would learn anything if the dons weren't Light Witches."

"But what does that sign mean?" Spike asked.

"I can only suppose it's all been caused by Wolfbane," Sir Chadwick sighed. "He's obviously gone into the past because he intends to alter something. Their counterparts at the Ministry of Time must have informed the Wizards at the Ministry of Coincidence. They've put what they call a Time Freeze on Speller until they can see how Wolfbane intends to alter the future. Nothing will happen here until the freeze is lifted. The sooner we get into the past and stop Wolfbane's mischief, the better."

The Time Witches

He smiled grimly at Captain Starlight. "There's nothing we can do here, Adam. I suggest we all go to London in the Atlantis Boat and stay in my rooms at the Alhambra Theater."

Abby looked up at him and said, "It *will* be all right, Sir Chadwick, won't it?"

He smiled at her reassuringly, but Abby thought he looked a little worried.

"Yes, Abby, everything will be all right in the end," he replied. But behind his back, Sir Chadwick had his fingers crossed.

15

Where the Wizards Work

The following morning, a silent group sat at breakfast around the dining table in Sir Chadwick's set of rooms, high in the Alhambra Theater, London. Only the Great Mandini had any appetite. In addition to his own, he had eaten both Abby and Spike's boiled eggs.

"I always eat when I am anxious," he explained, lest anyone should think him insensitive.

"Are you finished, sir?" murmured Shuffle, Sir Chadwick's servant.

"Yes, thank you," Sir Chadwick replied with a sigh. "You can take it away," he said, gesturing toward the untouched plate of bacon and eggs before him. Then he glanced at the window. "At least it's a bright day," he said more cheerfully. "I think we'll walk to the Ministry, Abby." He glanced at his pocket watch. "We'll leave in three minutes. Shuffle, bring Miss Abby's coat as well as my own, please."

"But it's a fine summer day," Abby protested.

"Just do as I say, child," Sir Chadwick replied gently.

Captain Starlight drank some more coffee and passed his own bacon to Benbow, who was perched on a bust of

Napoleon resting on a stand by the fireplace. "Good luck with the Wizards, Chadwick," he said gravely. "I'm sorry I'm not coming with you."

Sir Chadwick nodded. "So am I, but you know how precise they are about protocol. They said it must be Abby and me. If you came as well, Adam, it might endanger the application." He rose from his seat as Shuffle entered with their coats.

On the stroll down Shaftesbury Avenue, Sir Chadwick encountered several friends and acquaintances, but he didn't stop to chat as was his usual practice. "I really like London in good weather," he said as they passed the National Gallery.

Abby felt rather warm in her coat. "Where exactly is the Ministry of Time, Sir Chadwick?" she asked as they crossed Trafalgar Square.

"The bottom end of Whitehall," said Sir Chadwick, suddenly stopping in front of the statue of King Charles I mounted on a horse.

"Step in here," he said, gesturing toward the stone plinth.

"But that's solid stone," replied Abby, puzzled.

Sir Chadwick reached out and his hand disappeared into the plinth. "Not quite," he said, and they stepped inside.

They were in pitch-darkness. Suddenly, Abby felt herself turned upside down. She knew she was the other way up, but her feet still seemed to be standing on solid ground. Gravity must have reversed itself.

"Out we go again," said Sir Chadwick, and they passed through the stone once more. But now Abby found herself in a very different London.

It was snowing in the twilight of an early evening, and the sky was the color of lemons. People passing by wore very old-fashioned clothes. The women wore long skirts and the men top hats. There were no cars. All the traffic was horse-drawn, but the sound of hooves was muffled by thick snow.

"Aren't you glad you wore your coat now?" smiled Sir Chadwick.

"Where are we?" Abby asked.

"Wizard World," he replied.

"Why is it winter?"

Sir Chadwick pulled up the collar of his own coat before he answered. "Apparently, the Wizards kept the weather fine for about a thousand years, but they got bored with it at the beginning of the twentieth century and decided on a change. This is how London was in Edwardian times, more than a hundred years ago."

"I must say it looks very nice," said Abby. "The streetlamps look different."

"That's because it's gaslight. Pretty, isn't it?"

Sir Chadwick took her hand, and they plodded on through the snow until they arrived outside a huge gothic building close to Parliament Square. Abby recognized it from books as the Houses of Parliament.

"Do human beings exist here, too?" she asked.

Sir Chadwick shook his head. "Just Wizards. They live a great deal like human beings. Or, to be more precise, human beings live a great deal like Wizards. Humans don't realize it, but they've been imitating the Wizards throughout history."

Eventually, Sir Chadwick stopped in front of a tall, thin figure. Wearing a long greatcoat and a top hat, the man stood guard at the entrance of an imposing building. Soft lights glowed in its hundreds of windows.

The man touched the brim of his hat and behind him, a pair of massive, carved doors swung open. "Just up the flight of stairs on the left and along the corridor until you pass the marble bust of Merlin. The Permanent Undersecretary of Time is expecting you, Sir Chadwick, Miss Clover," said the doorman.

Abby looked at the man's face closely. It was extraordinarily narrow with a long, pointed nose and violet-colored eyes. But Abby would have sworn he was wearing false eyebrows, they were so unnaturally large and bushy. She was about to mention it to Sir Chadwick, but he anticipated her question and raised a finger to his lips.

They entered a cavernous hallway. Alcoves along the walls held statues of men. Although they were each dressed in clothes from different periods of history, all the men looked the same. They were all tall and very thin, just like the doorman they had just passed.

Their feet echoing on the marble floor, Sir Chadwick and Abby climbed the curving marble staircase and arrived in a corridor with a high vaulted ceiling that appeared to stretch as far as the eye could see. After trudging along for what seemed like ages, Abby said, "We're going to be late for our appointment at this rate."

"Oh, no," said Sir Chadwick, unconcerned. "Time doesn't exist inside the Ministry."

"Time doesn't exist inside the Ministry of Time," Abby replied. "That sounds very odd."

"Actually, it's called a paradox," Sir Chadwick answered.

"I like the sound of that word," said Abby. "I wish I knew what it meant."

"You will if you're around Wizards long enough," said Sir Chadwick with a sigh. Then he stopped. "Ah, the bust of Merlin."

Abby thought the marble head also looked like the doorman, except the carving had a long beard.

Sir Chadwick rapped on the door and a booming voice called out, "Come."

Abby had expected to enter a huge office, but the room in which they found themselves was quite small and cluttered with furniture. Leather couches and armchairs were crammed against a small, carved desk piled high with papers. The dark walls were crowded with portraits of important-looking long-faced men.

A tall figure, wearing a black jacket and striped trousers, stood with his back to them, jabbing at a blazing fire with a long poker. When he turned, Abby was surprised.

He looked just like all the statues and portraits, except for a pair of round wire-framed spectacles perched on the end of his long, pointed nose.

Sitting down behind the desk, he gestured for Sir Chadwick and Abby to sit down. Then he opened a file and studied it.

"So, Sir Chadwick, you and Miss Abby Clover wish to apply for a permit to travel back in time?" he said eventually.

"Actually, I did not intend to take Miss Clover with me," replied Sir Chadwick.

"Only two tickets are available and one is a half fare for a child. You must use them both," the man replied. "The rules are quite clear."

Sir Chadwick shrugged. "If you insist."

"And the purpose of this visit is to thwart the plans of Wolfbane, Grand Master of the Night Witches?" the Wizard continued.

"And to rescue my betrothed, Miss Hilda Bluebell, who has been abducted by Wolfbane."

The Permanent Undersecretary drummed his fingers and looked out of the window. "You do realize the Ministry of Coincidence has already taken certain steps in this matter?"

"I know they've put a Time Freeze on the town of Speller, but that doesn't get us anywhere," said Sir Chadwick, a trifle impatiently.

"So what is it that you actually intend to do?" asked the Wizard.

"Go back, rescue Miss Bluebell, put a stop to whatever Wolfbane intends to do, then return to the present."

"And how do you intend to stop Wolfbane?"

"I won't know until we get there," Sir Chadwick replied.

The Wizard drummed his fingers again. "When you say 'we,' you mean you and Miss Clover, of course?"

"Well, yes, but I would have preferred to take Captain Adam Starlight and the Great Mandini."

The undersecretary looked shocked. "Oh, no! We can't have all of you people blundering about in the past. Who knows what series of unforeseen events you'll set off? Miss Clover may accompany you. That is all."

"But —" began Sir Chadwick.

The Wizard held up a hand. "No *buts*, Sir Chadwick. You may have two return tickets for a duration of two weeks only — unless *we* decide to extend your stay. You will depart tomorrow morning and you will *not* stay past the time indicated on your return tickets." He held up a brown-paper envelope. "The details are all in here."

Sir Chadwick took the envelope and glanced inside before

returning his gaze to the undersecretary. "And what about a return ticket for Miss Bluebell?"

"Oh, yes, of course," said the undersecretary. "I almost forgot." And with a wintry smile, he took a sheet of paper and wrote a quick note. "This will do as a return ticket. Have it stamped by the doorman on your way out. Good evening."

"Don't you mean *good morning*?" asked Abby.

"It's any time you like here in the Ministry," said the Wizard, returning his attention to the pile of papers on his desk.

In the corridor outside the office, Sir Chadwick studied the contents of the envelope. "We're to depart from Torgate tomorrow morning," he said.

As they set off back along the corridor, Abby was sure she could hear distant laughter.

The doorman stamped Hilda's return ticket as the undersecretary had instructed. When they were outside in the snow again, Sir Chadwick let out a long sigh. "Curse their red tape," he exclaimed. "We really do need the others on such a perilous venture."

"I think they're coming anyway," said Abby.

"What do you mean?" asked Sir Chadwick.

Abby told him about the old photograph she and Spike had found, showing the Atlantis Boat tied up to Torgate Pier with Starlight, Mandini, and Spike aboard.

"Hmmm," said Sir Chadwick as they approached the statue of Charles I. "Now that *is* interesting."

16

Paddy the Pooka Returns

When Abby and Sir Chadwick returned to the Alhambra Theater, they found the others sitting in the stalls watching Sir Chadwick's company rehearsing a forthcoming production of *A Midsummer Night's Dream*. They slipped into the seats next to them.

Sir Chadwick's attention was immediately drawn to the work on the stage. He began to make notes on the production but was interrupted by a voice whispering in his ear.

"The fellow playing Bottom isn't up to *my* standard, Chaddy."

Startled, Sir Chadwick saw that Paddy the Pooka had materialized in the next seat. He was in his human form.

"My good chap," said Sir Chadwick, surprised. "I'm delighted you avoided the Time Freeze on Speller."

Paddy shrugged his shoulders. "We pookas don't care too much about Wizard rules, Chaddy. I thought it best to keep an eye on you in case that vile man, Wolfbane, tries any more of his villainy."

"That's most considerate of you," said Sir Chadwick, "but I really mustn't impose on your precious time."

"Think nothing of it, Chaddy, my dear," Paddy replied, patting him heavily on the shoulder. "But just now, I think I'll go and whisper a few suggestions to that fellow who's murdering Mr. Shakespeare's delightful words. I'll see you soon." And, with a slight popping sound, he vanished.

"Who were you talking to?" asked Captain Starlight, turning his attention from the stage.

Sir Chadwick shook his head. "Only another problem I have in my life," he answered. But then, to his astonishment, the actor playing the part of Bottom suddenly began to play his part with real verve.

Eventually, the cast broke off for lunch and Sir Chadwick led Starlight, Mandini, Spike, and Abby back to his rooms.

In Sir Chadwick's sitting room, he told them that the undersecretary had granted time travel permits for himself and Abby only.

Captain Starlight banged his fist on the table so hard the floorboards shuddered. The vibrations caused the bust of Napoleon to move slightly and Benbow opened one eye for a moment.

"Those Wizards are fools!" Starlight stormed.

"Yes," said Sir Chadwick. "But Abby has something interesting to tell us."

Abby told them of the old photograph she and Spike had found.

"That's right," said Spike. "I'd forgotten about that in all the excitement."

"What do you think it means?" asked Mandini.

Sir Chadwick leaned against the mantelpiece and looked thoughtful. "I think the Atlantis Boat can travel through time as well," he said eventually. "There's no other explanation."

"So, while you go back in the way the Wizards have chosen

for you, we three will be able to follow in the Atlantis Boat," Mandini said.

Sir Chadwick looked at them in turn. "It's asking a great deal, gentlemen," he said. "Abby and I are going with the permission of the Ministry of Time. You wouldn't be, and the Wizards can be very harsh with those who defy them."

"How harsh?" asked Spike.

"A thousand years in Lost Land is one of their lesser punishments."

They all looked thoughtful until Spike said, "Well, we know we're going because we've seen ourselves there, so there's not much point in worrying about it, is there?"

Abby looked toward Sir Chadwick. "Is that another paradox?" she asked.

"I think it is," he replied.

"Well, there's nothing useful we can do until tomorrow," said Captain Starlight. "How should we spend the time?"

Sir Chadwick shook his head. "Perhaps the rest of you would like to go out. I'm afraid I'm not very good company at the moment. I'm worried about Hilda."

"What will you do, Sir Chadwick?" asked Abby, concerned about her friend.

"I'll learn a part to take my mind off things," he replied briskly. "Jack Worthing in *The Importance of Being Earnest*, I think. It's a play I've never performed."

A thought suddenly occurred to Abby. "Sir Chadwick," she said. "Remember that time you put a spell on me so I would know the part of Wendy when we performed *Peter Pan*? Can't you do that for yourself?"

He nodded. "I don't actually know, child. It's a spell I've never quite been able to pull off for myself."

"Why do you think that is?" asked Spike.

Sir Chadwick scratched his red hair. "I can only suppose it's because Light Witches aren't supposed to help themselves with magic too much."

"Suppose I tried?" Abby said. "If I succeed, we could have a performance right here in the sitting room, just for ourselves."

Sir Chadwick looked doubtful. "Other Light Witches have attempted and failed, Abby. I hardly think a beginner . . ." His voice trailed off when he suddenly remembered how Abby had been able to recall the spirit of Ma Hemlock.

"Give it a try, Master," urged the Great Mandini.

Sir Chadwick looked brighter. "Very well," he said. "As you say, it's worth a try. But if the spell works on me, you'll all have to pitch in and help with the other parts. And *you'll* have to play one of the girls, Spike."

"I don't know if I'll be any good at that," said Spike, alarmed.

"It's an old tradition in the theater, my boy," said Mandini. "In Shakespeare's time, all the girls' parts were played by boys."

"Oh, all right, then," said Spike. "Anything for a laugh."

Abby thought for a moment and then chanted:

"Let Sir Chadwick know the play,
Take the part, and save the day."

"You didn't use any Ice Dust, Abby," said Spike.

But nobody else noticed his words, because, to Sir Chadwick's astonishment, he found that he already knew the role of Jack Worthing by heart!

"It's all up here, every line. Do you know what this means?"

he said triumphantly. "No more having to call on that quack Hissquick."

He was referring to a sorcerer who had caused him much trouble in the past when his spell had gone wrong and Sir Chadwick had been unable to cast off the role of Richard III.

Soon, when Sir Chadwick had performed the necessary spell on the others, they were ready to begin.

Abby's ruse to take Sir Chadwick's mind off his worries about Hilda worked splendidly. As they concentrated on the play, the person who surprised them all was Captain Starlight in the role of Lady Bracknell. When he delivered her famous line — *"A handbag!"* — even Benbow nodded his approval.

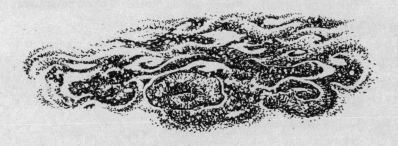

17

The Ride of a Lifetime

Early the following morning, they set off from London. Eventually, when Torgate came into sight, Captain Starlight stopped the boat, and Sir Chadwick stood before the controls.

"Boat," he said in a conversational voice. "Will you answer me a question?"

"If I know the answer, Sir Chadwick," the boat replied in a kindly voice.

"Can you travel back in time?"

"In certain circumstances."

"What would those be?"

"The purpose of the visit must be to do good."

"Will you take Captain Starlight, Mandini, and Spike into the past?"

The boat quivered slightly. "Let me look into their hearts," the boat voice said, and Abby watched in astonishment as the three of them momentarily glowed with a faint bluish light.

As the light faded, the voice said, "Their hearts are good. I will take them. Tell me the time and the place to which they wish to travel."

Sir Chadwick took out the envelope given to him by the undersecretary and read from one of the tickets. "To the ornamental floral clock on Torgate promenade, June 13, 1894, at precisely 9:44 A.M."

Sir Chadwick explained to the others, "That's where Wolfbane traveled to in the spectral carriage. He arrives exactly one minute later. If we all get there just before him, he'll be caught off guard. I will seize Hilda from him and spirit her aboard the Atlantis Boat."

"We'd better ask the Atlantis Boat to go to the pier. Then, when you've rescued Hilda, you can rush her to where we'll be waiting," said Starlight.

"Excellent planning," said Sir Chadwick. "Nothing can go wrong. Come along, Abby, it's time you and I were on our way." To Starlight and the others he said, "Once we're ashore, ask the boat to take you back in time."

"June 13, 1894, 9:44 A.M.," repeated Captain Starlight.

Sir Chadwick stood in the hatchway of the boat and struck an heroic pose. "Farewell, my friends, I wish us all good fortune." Then he and Abby stepped onto the beach and made for the steps to the promenade.

Abby picked her way cautiously over the sharp rocks and trod carefully on the oily steps. On the promenade, rain poured down on the windswept front and a shabby bus passed, splashing them with dirty rainwater.

All along the promenade, people stood huddled in doorways. Some, wearing plastic raincoats, trudged through the rain. Quite a few were munching hamburgers. Overhead, ugly concrete streetlights gave off a faint orange glare.

"This way," said Sir Chadwick, leading Abby past the ornamental flower clock with its bedraggled blooms. From somewhere ahead came the blaring sound of harsh electronic music, clashing disharmoniously with a wheezing pipe organ.

"Where are we going, Sir Chadwick?" Abby called out over the racket.

"Nearly there," he replied.

Abby crossed the road, hurrying after Sir Chadwick, until he stopped at the entrance to the fair. Gloomily, she looked up at the chipped paintwork and shabby signs on the attractions.

"Ah, that's what we want," said Sir Chadwick, leading her to a carousel.

It had obviously once been quite beautiful, but now the carved horses looked sadly neglected. Their prancing hooves were chipped and worn and, over the years, their ears had been knocked off, teeth broken, and saddles frayed.

The sign, RIDE OF A LIFETIME, had been badly repainted and half of its decorative lightbulbs were missing. Like the rest of Torgate, it was in a really sorry state. Abby and Sir Chadwick were its only customers.

Sir Chadwick glanced at her and said, "Oh, dear, in all the rush we forgot about your clothes."

"Won't these do?" said Abby, looking down at her fisherman's smock.

"Not for the year 1894," said Sir Chadwick. "I'm dressed in the height of fashion for that period," he said, gesturing to his wedding outfit of top hat and frock coat. "But your outfit won't do at all. Stand still," he instructed, placing a speck of Ice Dust on her head.

"*Martuvius,*" he muttered and, instantly, Abby's clothes were transformed.

She now wore a closely fitted white dress, long black stockings, and high-button boots. A wide-brimmed hat, decorated with frills, balanced precariously on her head, and a parasol was hooked over her arm.

"I can't wear all this," she gasped, clutching at the tight bodice. "I can barely move."

Sir Chadwick stroked his chin. "I see what you mean," he said and snapped his fingers.

Now, Abby stood before him wearing a sailor suit and a straw boater with a ribbon that hung down her back.

"Is that better?" he asked.

"Much better, thanks," replied Abby.

"We'd better get aboard quickly," Sir Chadwick instructed, glancing at his pocket watch. As soon as they mounted one of the shabby horses, the carousel began to spin.

Abby held onto the pole and watched Sir Chadwick clinging on precariously and fumbling as he tried to take the tickets from his waistcoat pocket with his free hand. The ride accelerated so quickly that Abby had difficulty breathing.

The carousel attendant appeared, balanced next to Sir Chadwick and examined the tickets. The man didn't seem bothered by the speed and, to Abby's astonishment, he looked very similar to the Permanent Undersecretary at the Ministry of Time. He appeared to be wearing a false nose!

The carousel whirled even faster and the attendant, disregarding the speed, hopped off lightly. The organ music continued to blare, and the whirling increased its momentum until Abby feared she would be flung off her wooden horse. Then the noise of the pipe organ faded and another sound replaced the discord.

First, she heard a growing roar, like a stormy sea crashing onto a rocky shore. Then a sound like a gale tearing through a great forest. Finally, it was as if thousands upon thousands of brass instruments were blowing the same rising note.

Abby could see nothing but a dim flickering light. Suddenly, all the colors of the rainbow flashed before her. Then she was dazzled by a white glare, so powerful she closed her eyes tight and clung to the pole with all her strength.

Just as she thought she could endure no more, she realized the ride was beginning to slow down. The carousel came to a stop, as Abby's breath returned and the music changed. Another pipe organ played "Oh, We Do Like to Be Beside the Seaside." Not only was the music in tune — it also sounded jaunty and very pleasant.

Abby felt sunshine on her face. She opened her eyes and saw she was on a totally different carousel from the one they'd started their journey on.

The ride was absolutely splendid. All the lights shone and the horses looked brand-new. They were freshly painted in silver and gold and had red-velvet saddles.

She felt quite cheerful, until a rough voice shouted, "Hey,

you two, what are you doing on that ride, don't you know it's broken?"

Abby and Sir Chadwick quickly got down.

A tall, thin man hurried toward them carrying a sign, which he propped up over Abby's vacated seat. It read:

THIS RIDE OUT OF ORDER
UNTIL FURTHER NOTICE

The man wore white trousers, a bowler hat, and a red-striped shirt with a spotted bow tie. He looked somehow familiar to Abby.

"Don't I know you?" she asked.

"Never seen you before in me life," replied the man hastily. "Now you clear off. I've got important things to do." And he hurried away into the fair.

Abby studied him as he made off, realizing that he looked the same as all the other men from the Ministry of Time, but for his large walrus mustache.

"Well, this is all a bit odd," said Sir Chadwick, still a little dazed. He glanced about him with growing astonishment and exclaimed, "My word, what an improvement!"

Abby was also enchanted by the sight of quite another Torgate.

Happy crowds thronged the promenade in the bright sunshine. The women looked splendid in long white dresses, their hats piled with artificial fruits and flowers. The men were mostly clad in brightly striped blazers, white flannel trousers, and straw boaters. Quite a lot of the children wore sailor suits, similar to the one Abby wore.

Most of all, Abby was thrilled by the vivid colors. The Torgate they had so recently left had been a dismal place. It had been like looking at the world through gray-brown darkened glass.

This Torgate glowed with light. A pink open-topped coach, drawn by white horses, glided past them to reveal the pier in all its glory. It was painted dark blue and silver, and the onion domes crowning the white Pavilion Theater were scarlet and gold. The sea beyond sparkled in bands of sapphire and indigo blue.

All along the promenade, baskets of red, purple, and yellow flowers hung from streetlamps, and the ornamental floral clock was a riot of color.

"We must hurry," said Sir Chadwick, "Wolfbane's carriage is due to appear by the floral clock in the next few seconds."

"What a shame," said Abby. "I would have liked to have stayed here for a while."

"No time, no time," replied Sir Chadwick, hurrying them forward. They crossed the road and stood opposite the ornamental clock.

"They should arrive any second," said Sir Chadwick, glancing again at his pocket watch. Abby strained forward in anticipation.

Seconds and then minutes passed, and all they saw were the strolling tourist crowds. But suddenly, people were stopping to watch a vehicle in the road.

Abby thought it might be Wolfbane, but, instead, an open coach approached. It was filled with men and women dressed in silk clothes. They were playing banjos and singing, "Come to the show on the end of the pier." A man shouted gaily. "Matinee performance at three o'clock. And again this evening at eight."

The Time Witches

They watched it pass and waited a bit longer until Sir Chadwick shook his head at Abby. "Something is wrong," he said. "They should have arrived by now."

Just then a boy walked by carrying an armful of newspapers.

"*Torgate Chronicle,*" he shouted. "Read all about it."

Sir Chadwick felt in the pocket of his money suit. "That's odd," he said. "It seems to be empty."

He glanced about him and noticed an old gentleman placing a newspaper carefully into one of the iron litter bins that lined the front.

Sir Chadwick waited until the man had moved away before he fished it out. He glanced quickly at the front page and exclaimed, with some feeling, "My word!"

"What is it?" asked Abby.

"It's the wrong date," said Sir Chadwick softly. "We're more than a month early. The carousel has brought us to the wrong time. Wolfbane isn't due for at least another five weeks. I wonder what the Wizards are up to."

18

Sir Chadwick Plays
The Corinthian

W ell, at least we're not too late," said Abby cheer-fully as they strolled along the promenade. "I don't mind waiting for a few weeks. Torgate looks wonderful. We can have a little holiday."

"We could," agreed Sir Chadwick, "if only we had some money."

"What about your money suit?"

Sir Chadwick turned the pockets inside out. "It doesn't seem to work in the past. More Wizard rules, I fear."

Abby racked her brains. "Perhaps we could make our way to Speller and borrow some money?"

Sir Chadwick shook his head. "No, Speller doesn't exist here, either. A Time Freeze works in the past as well."

"What are we going to do?" said Abby. "Can't you make a spell or something?"

"I'd rather not," he replied. "I was only permitted to bring one wandful of Ice Dust. We may need all of that for emergencies."

"So how will we live?" said Abby. "I'm beginning to feel quite hungry."

Sir Chadwick did not hesitate. "I saw a sign back at the fair that may be our salvation," he said. "Follow me."

They hurried back to the silent carousel and passed farther into the fair to where a sign proclaimed:

TEN POUNDS FOR ANYONE
WHO CAN STAY IN THE RING
FOR ONE THREE-MINUTE ROUND
WITH IRON FIST JONES

Beneath the challenge was a drawing of a ferocious-looking man wearing boxing gloves and a bathing costume. He was entirely bald and had the biggest muscles Abby had ever seen.

A large tent stood before them with the flap open. A fat man with bristling white sideburns and a bottle-green frock coat stood outside shouting through a megaphone. "Who dares? Who dares? Who dares stay in the ring for one round with Iron Fist Jones? Ten pounds to anyone who can face this man of metal and live to tell the tale."

"I accept your challenge," Sir Chadwick called out to the man.

Abby tugged at his sleeve and whispered, "Are you sure, Sir Chadwick?"

"We must eat, child," replied Sir Chadwick as they entered the tent. It was already crowded with spectators and so filled with cigar smoke the boxing ring was hardly visible in the blue haze.

While Sir Chadwick took off his coat and waistcoat and handed them to Abby, the fat man entered the ring and announced the challenge.

"Iron Fist Jones will fight . . ." He broke off and leaned toward Sir Chadwick. "What is your name, sir?"

"In sporting circles I am known as The Corinthian," replied Sir Chadwick calmly. The fat man nodded, then announced, "Iron Fist Jones will fight The Corinthian."

Another man handed Sir Chadwick a pair of boxing gloves. While he put them on, Iron Fist Jones entered the ring. He looked even more dangerous in the flesh than he did in the drawing outside the tent. Abby sat in Sir Chadwick's corner and watched Iron Fist Jones as he acknowledged the cheers and boos of the crowd.

The fat man called the contestants to the center of the ring, and a bell sounded. Abby could feel her heart in her mouth as the two circled each other. Iron Fist Jones lunged forward and shot his right fist out with alarming speed. Sir Chadwick just seemed to melt away from the blow.

Iron Fist tried to hit him three more times, then Sir Chadwick stepped forward. The following flurry of fists was little more than a blur to Abby and the rest of the spectators. When Sir Chadwick stepped back, Iron Fist Jones stood swaying with glassy eyes for a couple of seconds before crashing to the floor.

There was a moment's silence, then a roar of applause rose from the crowd. The fat man stepped forward in astonishment. By now, Sir Chadwick had pulled off his boxing gloves and was taking his clothes from Abby.

The fat man leaned over the unconscious Iron Fist Jones, saying, "Are you all right, my boy?"

The crowd chanted. "Count, count, *count!*"

Finally, and with great reluctance, the fat man began to count to ten. As he finished, Iron Fist Jones began to stir.

"Pay up, pay up!" shouted the crowd.

The fat man reached into his pocket and produced a small leather bag. With a flourish, he handed it to Sir Chadwick, who waved triumphantly to the cheering crowd.

"Be so kind as to give me a hand to get Iron Fist back to his dressing room, sir," the fat man pleaded.

"Certainly," replied Sir Chadwick, and they hauled the swaying boxer to his feet. Supporting him under each arm, they guided him to a seat in a distant part of the tent, away from the crowd.

Abby followed and watched as the fat man held smelling salts under Iron Fist's nose. Seeing that Jones was well on his way to recovering, Sir Chadwick was about to leave when the fat man put a restraining hand on his arm.

"A moment, sir, if you will?" he said quickly. "Allow me to introduce myself. I am Horace Greenbower, the owner of this attraction."

"Chadwick Street and Miss Abby Clover, delighted to make your acquaintance," replied Sir Chadwick.

Horace Greenbower held out both hands in a pleading gesture. "I have a confession to make," he said in a contrite voice. "I fear I have practiced a slight subterfuge upon you, sir."

"What does subterfuge mean?" asked Abby.

"A trick," said Sir Chadwick, opening the leather bag and examining the contents. "There's not ten pounds here," he said after a moment. "Just a lot of old pennies."

Horace Greenbower sighed. "I'm afraid Iron Fist Jones and I have fallen on hard times," he said in a broken voice.

Now it was Sir Chadwick's turn to sigh. "No dinner or rooms at the Grand Hotel for us after all, Abby," he said.

Horace Greenbower brightened suddenly. "If it's food and lodgings you require, sir, I can offer both. My credit is excellent at the Imperial Fried Fish Emporium, and Mrs. Green-bower runs a splendid boardinghouse that caters to those in the theatrical profession."

"Fish and chips it is, then," said Sir Chadwick, more brightly. "Lead on, Mr. Greenbower."

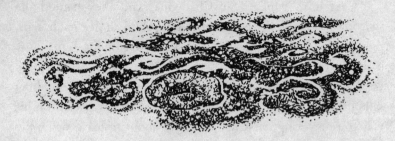

The Time Witches

19

Abby Meets the Little People

The Imperial Fried Fish Emporium turned out to be a splendid establishment. A large, airy room filled with tourists, the walls were clad in dark green marble and decorated with gold leaf, and the tables covered in snowy tablecloths. White-coated assistants stood behind the counter at three great fryers, and smartly dressed waitresses hurried cheerfully from table to table.

They sat in a window seat, each eating a plate of crispy golden fish and chips, as Horace Greenbower told Abby and Sir Chadwick of his troubles.

"I don't just run the boxing booth," Horace explained carefully. "I am also something of a theatrical manager. But unfortunately, my recent plans have gone somewhat awry. At great personal expense, I engaged an entertainer to star in the show at the Pavilion Theater at the end of the pier.

"He is Mr. Hamilton Coady, who possesses a fine tenor voice and also tap-dances in the American style. Sadly, he contracted laryngitis yesterday, and to cap it all he broke a leg."

"How did he break his leg, Mr. Greenbower?" asked Abby.

"Practicing his tap dancing in the hallway of the boardinghouse just after Mrs. Greenbower's maid had washed the marble floor."

"Unfortunate indeed," said Sir Chadwick.

Mr. Greenbower leaned forward, a forkful of chips halfway to his mouth. "I don't suppose I could interest you in a career in the boxing ring, sir?"

Sir Chadwick smiled but shook his head. "I must confess, Mr. Greenbower, I don't really approve of fisticuffs."

Iron Fist Jones put down his knife and fork. "Neither do I, sir. A nasty, brutal sport, if you ask me," he said with some feeling. "I always wanted to be a trapeze artist, but I had to give it up."

"Why, Mr. Iron Fist?" Abby asked.

"My timing was bad," he replied sadly. "I kept missing my catcher. Now my career as a boxer is over as well."

"Why, Mr. Iron Fist?" Abby asked again.

Mr. Greenbower answered. "His heart's just gone out of it. You're right, Jones, it's time to hang up the gloves."

"So you're all out of work," said Abby, pushing her empty plate aside.

"Not necessarily," replied Sir Chadwick with a contented smile. He looked at Mr. Greenbower. "Horace — may I call you Horace?"

"I would deem it an honor."

"And you must call me Charles. Charles Stanhope. It's my stage name." Sir Chadwick could see that Abby was looking puzzled, so he winked at her. "And Miss Abby Clover, here, is my ward."

"Delighted," said Horace with a half bow.

Sir Chadwick continued. "Horace, I have some talent as a singer and tap dancer in the American style."

"You do?" said Horace, sitting up with sudden interest.

"Certainly, and what is more, Miss Clover dances with great verve and is a virtual nightingale when it comes to a song."

"Am I?" said Abby, but no one was listening. Horace was slapping Sir Chadwick on the back with great enthusiasm. Only Iron Fist Jones looked despondent.

"Cheer up, Iron Fist," said Sir Chadwick, noticing how downcast he was. "I'll require a dresser, so you are employed again."

"In that case I'll have another round of fish and chips," he said cheerily.

"Perhaps my fortunes are changing at last," said Horace. "Another glass of beer, sir, and another glass of lemonade for Miss Clover — before we attend upon Mrs. Greenbower?"

"Delighted, old chap," replied Sir Chadwick, pushing his empty plate away.

The Sea View Guesthouse was just a short stroll along the promenade. It was a tall white building with a short flight of steps. Horace opened the door with his latchkey and called out, "It is I, precious one."

Mrs. Greenbower was descending the staircase with a tray when they entered. She was a pretty woman with ringlets and as stout as her husband.

"I've just been taking Mr. Coady his luncheon," she explained. "His injuries have not impaired his appetite."

"Allow me to introduce our new guests, my dear," said Horace, doffing his top hat. "My wife, Gloria Greenbower, Charles Stanhope and Miss Abby."

Mrs. Greenbower placed the tray on a hall table before giving a short curtsy. "Delighted, Mr. Stanhope," she said, and smiled at Abby. "And is this your daughter?"

"No," said Sir Chadwick. "Abby is my ward. Her parents are away on a long sea voyage."

"Well, you're most welcome, my dear," said Mrs. Greenbower. "Now, I've got a nice room for you, next to Mr. O'Grass and the Dancing Leprechauns."

"Dancing Leprechauns?" said Abby, intrigued.

"Pat O'Grass and His Dancing Leprechauns, a fine act," said Horace. "You will share the bill with them at the Pavilion Theater. As you may have guessed, Mr. O'Grass and the Dancing Leprechauns hail from the Emerald Isle."

Just then, there was the sound of chattering and laughter as seven little men came tumbling down the stairs, followed by a young man who was much taller. He wore a heavy beard and long sideburns. All were dressed in hairy green suits with hats pulled over their ears and each carried a knobbly walking stick.

"And here is Mr. O'Grass and his fellow artistes," said Horace. "I'll make the introductions."

After the handshakes, Mr. O'Grass said, "Sure, an' top o' the mornin' to you all. It's been grand to meet you, sure it has," and he hurried the little men out of the front door.

Mrs. Greenbower showed Sir Chadwick and Abby to the landing on the first floor and opened a door.

"This will be your living room," she said. "Your bedrooms are on either side."

The living room was airy with a wide bay window looking out over the sea. There were two comfortable armchairs, a small writing desk, a large Turkish carpet, and a table with a green baize tablecloth.

The wallpaper had an intricate pattern of roses, and there

were watercolor sketches of Torgate on the walls. Standing in the center of the table was a machine of a kind that Abby had never seen before.

"Delightful, Mrs. Greenbower," said Sir Chadwick with genuine pleasure.

"What's this, Mr. Greenbower?" asked Abby, pointing to the contraption.

"One of those newfangled telephones," Horace said with some pride. "We had a grand London impresario staying here for a few days and he insisted we have it installed."

"And where are your bags, my dears?" asked Mrs. Greenbower.

Sir Chadwick shrugged in resignation. "Lost on the train from London, I'm afraid. We'll have to buy new clothes and costumes, I fear, if we can get an advance on our salaries."

"Easily arranged. My credit is good everywhere. When you're ready, we can go shopping," said Horace. "Just give me a call. We're on the ground floor, at the back of the house."

When Abby and Sir Chadwick were alone, Abby said, "Why did you call yourself Charles Stanhope?"

Sir Chadwick smiled. "I don't want the name Sir Chadwick Street up in lights on the Pavilion Theater. It's just possible Wolfbane might see it."

"What about me?" said Abby. "He knows my name, too."

"Yes, you're right," said Sir Chadwick. "We'll have to work something out."

"And I don't think I can sing and dance, Sir Chadwick, at least not on the stage," she added, but Sir Chadwick held up his hand and began to search through his pockets.

Eventually, he took two items from his coat and lay them

on the table. The first was a thick little book, which he began to thumb through.

"What's that?" asked Abby.

"My millennium diary," he answered, still concentrating on the book. "Ah, I see my previous self is appearing in the West End at the moment." Then he picked up the other item. "My folding wand," he said, flicking it open to check the contents.

"Precious little Ice Dust in one wandful, I'll have to be sparing in its use." He smiled at Abby. "Now, what were you saying about not being able to perform onstage?"

While he spoke, he waved the wand over her head.

"It's just that I don't know how to sing and dance," Abby repeated. "I could always make myself invisible. The audience might think it was a magic trick."

"No need to worry on that score," said Sir Chadwick. "Help me roll back the carpet."

Once it was done, a large area of bare floorboards was revealed. "Watch me do this," he instructed. "And then you repeat it."

Sir Chadwick executed a marvelous tap dance, his feet drumming rhythmically upon the bare boards.

"I don't think I can remember all that," said Abby doubtfully. "It's not like acting."

"Just trust my spell," he answered. "And I'll want you to sing at the same time."

"Sing! Sing what?"

"Take a seat and I'll dash something off," he replied and, sitting at the little desk, he began to scribble rapidly.

Abby looked out of the window at the beach until Sir Chadwick cleared his throat. "What do you think of this?" he said, and began to recite.

"Come, lads and lasses, cast thy sloth,
Cut your clothes to suit your cloth,
When summer meadows summon lovers,
Sweet sunshine shall be your covers."

Abby looked a bit doubtful. "It sounds a bit Shakespearean for a seaside song, don't you think?"

Sir Chadwick took the sheet of paper. He studied it for a moment and nodded. "Perhaps you're right," he said. "Give me another few minutes."

Abby continued to gaze out of the window until Sir Chadwick said, "By Jove, I think I've got it." He hummed a few bars and made some alterations. Finally, he handed the new version to Abby, saying, "What do you think of this?"

Abby read aloud:

" *'Sunshine Millionaire' by Charles Stanhope*

"If your dreams aren't worth a cent,
And you ain't got next week's rent,
Take a tip from Mr. Sun,
He's not blaming anyone.
When the skies are filled with gray,
He just waits another day.

"Mr. Sun knows things will alter,
So keep your chin up, never falter,
Better days are on their way,
Blues are never here to stay.

"I'm a sunshine millionaire,
I've got sunshine wealth to spare,

Tell you how I made my pile,
I put sunshine in my smile.
Rich men try to buy my secret,
Don't want their money, they can keep it.
They don't see that life is fun,
Imitating Mr. Sun."

Abby looked up, impressed. "That's really good, Sir Chadwick," she said. "You are clever."

Sir Chadwick looked pleased. "I gave it an American flavor," he said. "I thought we would bill ourselves as coming straight from the New York stage."

"It may take me a little while to learn the song," said Abby.

Sir Chadwick smiled. "Just try to sing and dance. As I said, you'll be surprised."

"Well, if you say so," said Abby. "Here goes."

To her astonishment, Abby found that she could tap-dance.

"Now sing," called out Sir Chadwick.

"But I don't know the tune," she replied.

"Yes, you do," he answered, and he was right. Abby found herself singing a catchy melody she had never heard before.

"You were wonderful, my dear," Sir Chadwick said, when Abby finished her performance.

"I agree with you, Chaddy," said another voice, and with a popping sound Paddy the Pooka appeared. He had a human body, but still wore his donkey head. He raised his hat and said, "Great to see you, Abby Clover."

"Hello again, Mr. Pooka," replied Abby, taking his hairy hand.

"Just Paddy, darlin'," he said, laughing. Then he spoke to Sir

Chadwick. "I thought I'd better warn you, Chaddy, that Pat O'Grass fella is about as Irish as the Rock of Gibraltar."

"Really?" said Sir Chadwick. "I had no idea."

"Just listen to his accent," continued Paddy. "There's something strange going on here. Keep your eyes open." And, with a wink to Abby, he vanished with another popping sound.

"How did he manage to travel back through time?" asked Abby.

Sir Chadwick raised his hands in resignation. "Pookas can follow the person they're attached to anywhere, even through time, if necessary. It's most disturbing, the way he keeps appearing like that."

"How long will he go on following you?" asked Abby.

"I understand it's until he's done me a very big favor."

"That's puzzling," said Abby. "You would expect pookas to follow you around until you did *them* a big favor."

"Don't try and apply logic to the behavior of a pooka, child," sighed Sir Chadwick. Then he tapped the bare boards. "Let's try a few more dances before we go shopping with Horace."

20

The Detective Hunting Pat O'Grass

An enthusiastic Horace Greenbower took Abby and Sir Chadwick to a costume shop in one of the narrow lanes near the station.

"I'm surprised you have such a shop in Torgate," Sir Chadwick remarked.

"Oh, we get some pretty big acts at the Pavilion Theater," Horace replied. "And a couple of the big hotels often have fancy-dress balls."

The costumes they chose for their act were splendid.

Sir Chadwick selected a top hat and a silk suit made from the Stars and Stripes, and a small goatee beard to go with it. He had decided to appear as Uncle Sam.

He chose a white flouncy dress for Abby and a curly blond wig. "Blond children always go down well with a Victorian audience," he explained. "They are notorious for their sentimentality. We'll bill you as Mary Goodheart."

"All right," said Abby reluctantly. "But I'm only going to wear it on the stage."

Next, Horace took them to a department store, where his credit was also good, to buy them some daytime clothes.

Sir Chadwick selected a cream-colored three-piece suit and some shirts. Abby insisted on another sailor outfit.

"And we'll need bathing suits and a bucket and spade for Abby," said Sir Chadwick. The assistant agreed to deliver their purchases to the guesthouse.

"I have arranged for an audition with the manager of the Pavilion Theater," said Horace as they left the store. "He awaits meeting you with eager anticipation."

Horace had exaggerated slightly. They had a brief meeting with a rumpled-looking man, who was appropriately called Mr. Rush. He could hardly stand still for a minute. "Excellent, excellent, Mr. Stanhope, Miss Goodheart," he called out after listening to only one song. "Can you go on tonight?"

"Of course," replied Sir Chadwick. "But first you must discuss our remuneration with our agent, Mr. Horace Greenbower."

Sir Chadwick had been right when he'd predicted the audience would like Abby's song. That evening, after the first performance, they cheered and cheered and demanded an encore. Abby had to sing the song three times.

She also enjoyed the rest of the show. The magician wasn't as good as the Great Mandini, but he let her play with his white rabbit when it wasn't needed in the act. And she particularly liked Pat O'Grass and His Dancing Leprechauns. They sang Irish ballads and did jigs that sounded like rolling thunder as their little boots pounded on the bare boards of the stage.

The following day, Charles Stanhope and Mary Goodheart received ecstatic notices in the local paper. "Brilliant . . . outstanding . . . wonderfully gifted," Sir Chadwick read aloud from his deck chair on the sand as Abby busied herself, making a massive sand castle in the shape of the king of Lantua's palace.

Abby looked up and glanced at the happy families all around her on the golden beach. "Isn't it a pity that Torgate can't stay like this forever, Sir Chadwick?" she said.

"I couldn't agree more, child," he replied, pushing his tweed hat over his face to protect it from the hot sun.

And so the days began to pass. At the end of the first week, Mr. Rush asked Sir Chadwick if he and Abby could add a one-act melodrama on the evils of drink to their repertoire. Sir Chadwick was delighted with the request and the new little play was added to their performance without a hitch.

Abby's song became a big hit with the tourists, and soon people were singing it everywhere. The pianist in the Darkwood Arms played it several times each evening, and it became a favorite with the passengers on the open-topped coaches.

After the performance each evening, Abby, Sir Chadwick, and the other performers at the Pavilion Theater would go to the Imperial Fried Fish Emporium and have a late supper. Then Sir Chadwick would escort Abby to the guesthouse, where Mrs. Greenbower would see her into bed while Sir Chadwick, Iron Fist Jones, and Horace went for a drink at the Darkwood Arms, a bar near the fair.

Sometimes, when he was free, Pat O'Grass would go with them, but only for a quick drink. After that he would return to Mrs. Greenbower's guesthouse to make sure the little folk were all right.

Abby slept late in the mornings and after lunch went to the beach with Sir Chadwick. He snoozed in a deck chair while she swam in the sea. She got very brown and became quite an expert at building sand castles.

After some very pleasant weeks, on June 12, the day before Wolfbane and Hilda were due to arrive from the future, a curious thing happened.

The weather was blazing hot. Indeed, it was so hot that Sir Chadwick bought a large Panama straw hat to protect his face while he sat in his customary deck chair. Abby was building a sand castle at his feet.

They both looked up at the same time and saw a large man with a brush mustache. He was wearing a thick black suit and bowler hat and was plodding through the crowds toward them, mounted on one of the donkeys that were for hire on the beach.

Even from a distance, Abby could see his red complexion and the perspiration streaming down his face. As he drew level with Sir Chadwick, the man gave a moan and slid from the donkey's back in a dead faint.

Sir Chadwick leaped up and knelt by the man's side. "Bring me some seawater in your bucket, Abby," said Sir Chadwick, loosening the man's tie and unbuttoning his stiff white collar.

Abby returned with the seawater, and Sir Chadwick dripped some of it onto the man's face with his own spotted red handkerchief. After a moment, the man revived and Sir Chadwick helped him to the empty deck chair next to his own.

"Thank you, sir," he said in a hoarse voice with a northern accent. "I'm afraid I've been overdoing it a bit."

"Best to take it easy in weather like this, old chap," said Sir Chadwick.

"Can't do that, sir — can't do that. I'm hot on a trail."

"A trail?" said Sir Chadwick.

"Hunting a villain." The man looked about him and continued, "If you're from these parts, perhaps you've seen him."

The stranger took a piece of paper from his jacket pocket and handed it to Sir Chadwick. "I wonder if you recognize this man?" he asked.

Sir Chadwick studied the sheet of paper, then looked up and said, "And who are you, sir?"

The man took out a card and handed it to Sir Chadwick, saying, "Sorry, I should have introduced myself."

Sir Chadwick read the card aloud. "Cecil Entwhistle. Private Investigator. So you're a detective, Mr. Entwhistle. And why are you looking for this man?"

"It's a confidential matter," he replied. "But I can say he's a very desperate character. And he did a great deal of damage to some property that is owned by the gentleman who employs me."

"Well, I can't say that I recognize him from this picture," said Sir Chadwick and he handed the paper to Abby with a warning wink. "How about you, child?"

Taking the hint from Sir Chadwick's wink, Abby glanced at the picture, shook her head, and continued to build her latest sand castle.

Mr. Entwhistle took back his card and the picture. "Well, if you were to see him, sir, perhaps you would call on me. I'm staying at the Metropole Hotel, room twenty-seven." As he was about to remount his donkey, he paused. "I might add there is a large reward for the apprehension of this gentleman."

"What's his name?" asked Sir Chadwick.

"Jack Elvin," replied Entwhistle. "And to repeat myself, he's a very dangerous character. Good day to you."

As the donkey walked away it turned its head for a moment and winked at Abby. She knew in an instant that it was Paddy the Pooka! He had deliberately brought the detective to them.

Abby could hardly breathe from excitement. The detective had said the name *Jack Elvin*. It was her great-great-grandfather. And what was more, despite the heavy beard he now wore, the clean-shaven man in the picture was clearly Pat O'Grass!

21

A Telephone Call Changes Things

Back in their sitting room at the guesthouse, Sir Chadwick sat down in an armchair, deep in thought. "It all seems to be getting very complicated," he murmured eventually.

"Very complicated," agreed Abby.

Sir Chadwick sat forward in his chair and said, "Why did we get here at the wrong time? The Wizards don't usually make a mistake like that. But all these complications look like their work, right enough."

Then, for the first time since they had been in the rooms, the telephone on the table rang. Abby and Sir Chadwick exchanged glances and Sir Chadwick gingerly picked up the receiver.

From where she sat by the window, Abby could hear a rasping voice on the other end. "This is the Ministry of Coincidence, Permanent Undersecretary to the Minister speaking. Please will you bring the man calling himself Pat O'Grass to the telephone?"

"Certainly," replied Sir Chadwick. Then he said to Abby, "Would you tell Mr. O'Grass he's wanted on the telephone?"

Abby ran along the corridor and knocked on his door. When

she heard O'Grass ask, "Who's there?" she called out, "There's an urgent telephone call for you in our room, Mr. O'Grass." Before he could answer, she ran back to the sitting room.

O'Grass followed her and picked up the receiver. "Listen carefully," rasped a voice. "We know who you are and why you are on the run. Now, tell Sir Chadwick Street and Abby Clover why you are in hiding." Then the person calling hung up.

O'Grass slowly put down the telephone and looked imploringly at Sir Chadwick. "Do you happen to know anyone called Sir Chadwick Street, Mr. Stanhope?"

"Actually, that's me," said Sir Chadwick. "Charles Stanhope is my stage name."

"Did you hear what that voice said?" he asked.

Sir Chadwick nodded, and O'Grass sat down in a chair and buried his face in his hands. When he lifted his head again, he had removed his false beard to reveal a pleasant, open face, although it looked a trifle strained.

"Sir Chadwick," he said in a low voice. "Do you believe in elves?"

Sir Chadwick's expression did not alter. "I think there is some evidence to suggest they might exist," he said evenly.

"Really?" said O'Grass eagerly, and Abby noticed that his Irish accent had gone. "What would you say if I told you that my leprechauns aren't midgets, as everyone believes, but that they're actually elves, with some very strange powers?"

Sir Chadwick stood up and said, "I think I would ask you to stay to tea, sir, and tell us everything."

Just then, Mrs. Greenbower opened the door and stood looking bewildered. "Now what did I come up here for, Mr. Stanhope?" she said. "It was as if something told me you wanted me."

"Could we have tea for ten, please, Mrs. Greenbower?" said Sir Chadwick briskly.

"Ten?" said O'Grass when Mrs. Greenbower had hurried away.

"I thought you might want to invite the elves as well. I understand they're very fond of teatime."

"How do you know that?" asked O'Grass.

"Oh, I've had dealings with elves before," said Sir Chadwick.

O'Grass and the elves were coming into the living room as the tea arrived. Abby made sure everyone had a cup and a share of the sandwiches and cakes. The elves sat on the floor and began to chatter among themselves.

Their language was unlike anything Abby had ever heard. It sounded like leaves rustling in the wind, with an odd note like a birdsong and the occasional tinkling of running water. Occasionally, they would look at Abby and smile shyly.

"They like you," said O'Grass. "I can speak a bit of their language, and they're saying they know you're a friend."

"I'm very honored," said Abby. "I like them, too."

Pat O'Grass translated and Sir Chadwick held up a hand. "Perhaps we can all use a common tongue, gentlemen. And by the way, may we call you by your proper name, Mr. Elvin?"

Jack Elvin let out a long sigh of relief. "So you don't think I'm mad?"

Sir Chadwick shook his head and took a sip of his tea before replying. "On the contrary. But please, you must begin at the beginning and tell us how you got into all this trouble."

Abby looked very carefully at Jack Elvin and went to sit close by him.

Jack Elvin put down his cup and began. "I'm an engineer and an architect, Sir Chadwick, or at least I was. A plain chap who believed in facts and figures, bricks and mortar. Things you could touch and see."

Sir Chadwick nodded and Jack Elvin continued.

"Well, one day I got an invitation to visit Sir Morden Hardcastle, a baronet and industrial magnate in my part of the world up north."

At the name *Hardcastle*, the elves began to mutter in their own language again until Jack held a finger to his lips to silence them.

"What's an industrial magnet?" asked Abby.

"A *magnate*, Abby, is a rich and powerful man," said Sir Chadwick, nodding for Jack Elvin to continue.

"Sir Morden Hardcastle had an engineering project he engaged me to undertake. He wanted me to build a new steelworks in the valley he owned. The valley was beautiful, Sir

Chadwick. There was a forest, rolling farmland, and a stream that ran through it all.

"Sir Morden had built a house at the top end of the valley. The view was superb, but his house was hideous. It was a great ugly thing covered in green and brown tiles. It looked like a great toad squatting there.

"He wanted me to dam the stream, blow up the forest, and clear a level site to build a blast furnace. Well, it was his valley and he wouldn't be sharing it with anyone, so, reluctantly, I set about surveying the ground." Jack paused here and took another cucumber sandwich before resuming his story.

"When I was surveying the forest, strange things began to happen. My instruments would vanish. Birds would come and sit on my shoulders, and wild animals would visit me. And all the time, I thought I was being watched. Then one day, I saw the elves."

He gestured toward the little men who sat around his feet. They nodded in agreement and one of them stood up.

"My name is Lupin," he said in a high musical voice. "And my friends are called Gooseberry, Bramble, Acorn, Foxglove, Apple, and Chestnut in your language. We decided to confide in Jack Elvin because we knew he was kind. We told him the truth about Sir Morden Hardcastle. He is a cruel man, Sir Chadwick. He knew about us and he had been hunting us on his land."

"But surely a human being can't hurt an elf, Lupin," said Sir Chadwick.

"They can if they're a changeling," replied Lupin.

Sir Chadwick nodded. "Oh, I see. That does alter things."

"What's a changeling, Lupin?" asked Abby.

Lupin scratched his head before he answered. "Someone who doesn't know they are actually the child of Night Witches," he said. "Sometimes, Night Witches steal a human child and put one of their own in its place. They enchant the parents so they won't notice the difference. The changeling grows up thinking it is a human child, but they always turn out to be wicked. Sometimes they become Night Witches when they get older."

"So, Sir Morden Hardcastle was able to hunt you because he had evil powers he didn't even know he possessed?" said Sir Chadwick.

"Yes, yes," chorused all the elves.

"Couldn't you have just moved as far away as possible from this horrible man?" asked Abby.

Lupin shook his head. "Our elfberry tree was in the forest," he answered.

"Elfberry tree?" said Abby, puzzled.

Sir Chadwick interjected. "Elves must have elfberries in their diet to live, Abby," he explained. "The trees are very rare and only grow in certain forests."

"So what did you do?" asked Abby.

Jack Elvin smiled grimly. "I blew up his house instead of the forest," he said with a certain amount of satisfaction. "After that, I knew he would try to destroy me as well as the elves, so we gathered as many elfberries as we could carry with us, got up these disguises, and went on the run."

"And what made you come here?" asked Abby.

Jack Elvin shrugged. "I don't know. I'd never even heard of the place. It was as if something was compelling me to come to Torgate."

"And why did you choose to go on the stage?" said Sir Chadwick. "It does tend to be a choice of profession that will get you noticed."

Jack Elvin looked about him. "I would have attracted attention if I'd turned up anywhere with these seven little chaps, but in show business, the unusual is often the usual."

"I think that's another paradox," said Abby to the elves. "I'm beginning to get the hang of them now."

"So where are your families hiding?" asked Sir Chadwick. "Your wives and your children."

"Merlin College, Oxford. The Light Witch dons gave them sanctuary in the grounds of the college, but they couldn't take us all and the supply of elfberries is dwindling fast. As soon as we find somewhere else to live, we'll bring them to our new home."

Sir Chadwick stood up. "Well, thank you for telling us all this, gentlemen." He nodded to Jack Elvin. "But I must warn you, there is a man close on your trail."

"The detective Entwhistle?" asked Jack.

"Yes."

Jack looked about him, as though the man might actually be in the room. "He's been after us all along. I didn't know he was so close."

Sir Chadwick smiled. "I'm afraid that false beard doesn't help."

Jack held it up. "I know, but I can't grow a proper one. There seems to be a big gap in my chin where the hair doesn't grow well."

"Perhaps I can help," said Sir Chadwick. "Stand up."

Jack stood before Sir Chadwick and thrust out his chin. Sir Chadwick opened the end of his folding wand and took a single particle of Ice Dust in the palm of his hand. He rubbed his palms together and then lay his hands on Jack's chin. Immediately, a huge beard sprouted from Jack's face.

The hair was so long it brushed the floor.

"Oops," said Sir Chadwick. "I'd better adjust that. Now, let's see." He waved his hand in front of Jack's face, and the beard changed several times until it assumed a shape that won Sir Chadwick's approval. "That'll do," he said. "And you won't ever need to trim it."

Jack went to a mirror over the fireplace and studied his reflection. "You can do magic," he said to Sir Chadwick. "The elves said you could. What exactly are you?"

Sir Chadwick drew himself up and suddenly looked rather splendid. "I am Grand Master of the Ancient Order of Light Witches," he answered. "And you and your companions are now under my protection. Go back to your rooms for the time being. I will let you know what to do when I have decided on a course of action."

"Thank you, Sir Chadwick," said Jack. "You have no idea what a relief it is to have an ally." He and the elves lined up to shake hands before they trooped away. Abby smiled a special secret smile as she shook Jack's hand.

Sir Chadwick sat down in his chair again. "I wonder what is going to happen to them," he said thoughtfully.

"Well, according to my great-great-grandmother Mary Bowsprit's diary, Jack Elvin is going to meet her father, Josiah Bowsprit, at Speller station at eleven o'clock on the morning of June 17," said Abby.

Sir Chadwick sat up and looked at her sharply. "How do you know that?"

"My father read me some of Mary's diary," she explained.

"You're quite sure?" said Sir Chadwick intently.

"Absolutely," said Abby. "And you're right about all the co-incidences. It's odd that Hilda lived here in Torgate, isn't it?"

"Hilda lived here?" repeated Sir Chadwick, astonished.

"Yes, didn't you know? She told me when she was being fitted for her wedding dress."

"I had no idea," said Sir Chadwick softly. "The first time I met Hilda was when Michael Dillon, the manager of the Alhambra Theater, hired her." He felt in his pockets and found his millennium diary.

"Yes," he said. "Here is my entry for June 14, 1894: Mr. Dillon has hired a young lady for the company. She is very pretty and shows great promise."

He looked up. "All this means something, Abby. I feel unseen forces are definitely manipulating us. It's clearly the work of the Wizards. I do wish they wouldn't be so obscure."

"I did think it was odd that we hadn't seen her. I've been keeping an eye out," said Abby.

"That's probably Wizard work as well," said Sir Chadwick testily. "You do know what this means?"

"What?"

"When Wolfbane arrives here from the future, there will be two Hildas in Torgate. A very dangerous situation, indeed. We mustn't let them meet."

"Why not?" asked Abby.

"We shouldn't know what's going to happen to us in the future. It leads to terrible complications."

He sat at the table with his diary and began to make notes, which he read aloud. "Wolfbane kidnapped Hilda and took her back to June 13, 1894."

"Only he hasn't arrived yet because we came early and it's

The Time Witches

still only June 12," said Abby. "The Atlantis Boat is also due to arrive tomorrow."

Sir Chadwick nodded. "Hilda went to the Alhambra Theater in London on June 14, 1894 and was hired by Michael Dillon." He looked up again. "And you say that Jack Elvin meets Josiah Bowsprit on June 17?"

"Yes, and there's another date we've got to worry about," said Abby.

"What's that?" said Sir Chadwick.

Abby looked from the window at the pier glittering in the sunlight. "According to the records, there is going to be a great storm on June 15 and the pier is going to be blown away."

"I'd forgotten that," said Sir Chadwick with some feeling. "That's all we need."

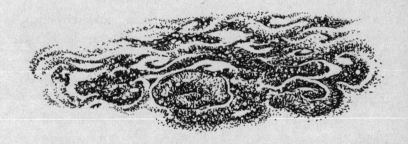

22

The Right Place at the Wrong Time

On the following morning, June 13, 1894, at precisely 9:40 A.M. according to Sir Chadwick's silver pocket watch, Abby, Sir Chadwick, Jack Elvin, and the seven elves stood on the promenade opposite the floral clock, waiting for the spectral carriage to materialize.

Knowing how Night Witches feared being tickled by elves, Sir Chadwick had recruited the little men to help rescue Hilda.

There were just five minutes to go before Wolfbane was due to appear. It was another beautiful day with a hint of clouds on the horizon.

"Now, you elves know what to do, don't you?" said Sir Chadwick.

"Tickle the Night Witches," chorused Lupin, Bramble, Gooseberry, Apple, Acorn, Foxglove, and Chestnut.

"I'm going to tickle them so hard they'll age by two hundred years before they know it," said Bramble fiercely. He was even smaller than the others and knew that when Night Witches were made to laugh they grew older and older.

"Me, too," shouted all the others.

Pleased by the elves' spirit, Sir Chadwick looked toward the others.

Abby confirmed their plan. "When the spectral carriage appears opposite the floral clock, I'll run forward and throw a handful of Ice Dust in the faces of the horses. That will stop them."

Sir Chadwick continued. "Then I shall throw Ice Dust over Wolfbane and snatch Hilda from his grasp."

Lupin joined in. "That's when we jump into the coach and tickle Wolfbane and his mother while you make your escape."

"Are you quite sure it won't be dangerous for the elves?" asked Jack anxiously.

Sir Chadwick laughed. "To be tickled by elves is the one thing Night Witches dread more than anything else."

"It's quite true," said Abby. "Believe me, I've seen it happen. The Night Witches howl horribly."

Sir Chadwick took out his pocket watch again. "Two minutes to go," he said. "Everybody ready?"

"Ready, Sir Chadwick," they all chanted in unison.

As the moment approached, Sir Chadwick, still concentrating on his watch, began to call out, "Four seconds, three seconds, two seconds, one second. Now!"

And nothing happened.

A milk cart, three hansom cabs, and an open-topped coach trundled past. But there was no sign of Wolfbane and Ma Hemlock's spectral carriage.

Sir Chadwick looked around wildly and consulted his watch again. Then he stopped a tall, thin man who was hurrying by.

"Excuse me," said Sir Chadwick, too agitated to notice that the thin stranger looked remarkably like a Wizard. "Can you please tell me the time?"

The thin man glanced at his watch and, keeping his head turned away, said, "Nearly ten-thirty," as he hurried on.

"Ten-thirty!" shrieked Sir Chadwick. "My watch is wrong. We're too late." He looked around in horror. "That means Wolfbane has already arrived."

Suddenly, Abby saw a familiar figure walking briskly along the opposite pavement. "Look, Sir Chadwick," she called out. "It's Hilda."

Sir Chadwick followed her pointing finger and saw Hilda Bluebell hurrying along the promenade. He shouted to Jack Elvin and the seven elves, "We'll see you back at the guesthouse." Then to Abby, "Come on, after Hilda."

Dodging through the traffic, they crossed the road and set off in the same direction as Hilda. Sir Chadwick saw the flowers of her hat ahead and slowed down to take hold of Abby's arm. "I've just thought of something," he said breathlessly.

"What's that?" replied Abby, hopping up and down in hope of seeing Hilda's hat.

"That may be the Hilda who was already here," he said.

"Yes," said Abby, "you could be right."

"In that case we must take care. We will be complete strangers to her. If we rush up and begin talking to her, she won't know what to think."

Abby slowed down. "I see what you mean." Then she had an idea. "But if she does recognize us, then we will know she's the Hilda from our future."

Sir Chadwick nodded. "Quite right," he said. "We shall reveal ourselves casually to her. If she doesn't recognize us, we will know which one she is."

They hurried on.

But on the promenade, events had taken another turn. Sir Chadwick's watch had been altered so as to be too early, not too late! The passing stranger who looked like a Wizard had given him quite the wrong time.

As a brewer's dray, pulled by two plodding shire horses, headed toward the Darkwood Arms, the lead horses suddenly reared back in alarm when an unexpected vehicle materialized in front of them.

It was Wolfbane in the spectral carriage, holding an unconscious Hilda in his arms. Opposite him sat his mother, pretending concern. The ghostly horses and coachman now had about them the illusion of flesh.

"Stop," shouted Wolfbane, and the coachman pulled up.

"This young lady is sick," Wolfbane called out to a workman on the promenade who seemed interested.

"There used to be a pharmacist just over there, sir, but I think it's closed," said the workman. "Do you want a hand?"

"I can manage," said Wolfbane and, carrying the still unconscious Hilda in his arms, he swept across the road. Lucia followed him into the shop that the workman had indicated. It was the premises he had located from Sid Rollin's files in the future.

The workman watched his progress and then turned back to look at the carriage Wolfbane had abandoned.

It had vanished!

He pushed back his cap and scratched his head for a moment and then, with a shrug, continued along the promenade. No one else seemed to have noticed anything odd.

23

The Atlantis Boat Arrives

Unaware of Wolfbane's arrival on the promenade, Abby and Sir Chadwick continued to follow the other Hilda in the flowery hat. Eventually, she turned into the street where the smartest shops in Torgate were located, and entered a large clothing store.

They paused outside and watched through the window as she removed her hat and took her place behind a counter.

"Come on," said Sir Chadwick, taking a deep breath.

As they entered the store, Hilda looked up and gave them a passing glance, but it was clear she did not recognize them. It seemed very strange to Abby. It was all she could do not to call out a greeting to her friend.

"I'd like to watch her for a moment," murmured Sir Chadwick, so they stopped, fairly close to Hilda, in front of a counter that sold gloves. After a moment, a haughty young man approached them.

"I would like to see some cotton gloves," said Sir Chadwick, "and also a pair for my young ward here."

"Any particular colors, sir?" asked the assistant with a slight sniff.

"Bring me all you have," said Sir Chadwick. "Then I'll make up my mind."

The assistant began to pile selections of gloves in front of Sir Chadwick, who pretended to examine them in great detail.

As they continued to sort through the pile, they could hear the conversation going on between Hilda and two other young lady assistants.

"Do you want to come to the Aquarium with us this evening, Hilda?" one asked. "They've got a new octopus on display. It looks ever so funny with all those little arms waving about."

"No, thank you, Elsie," Hilda replied, not looking up from the drawer of handkerchiefs she was arranging. "I'm going to the theater."

"Hilda's too good for us," said the girl called Elsie. She nudged the other assistant and said, "Hilda's going to be an actress, you know."

Hilda sighed. "I just said I'd like to be an actress, Elsie. I don't think there's much chance of its happening here in Torgate."

Elsie winked at the other girl and took a ring off her finger. Behind Hilda's back, she concealed it in a tray of spools of cotton.

"Oh, dear," said Elsie. "I've lost my ring. Has anyone seen it?"

Without looking around, Hilda continued to arrange the handkerchiefs. But she said, "Try under the blue cotton thread. I think I saw it there."

"Oh, yes," said Elsie. Then she smiled slyly to the other girl and said, "Hilda's mother must have been a witch. Was she a witch, Hilda?"

Hilda looked up. "I don't know who my mother was, Elsie. I'm an orphan. I told you that before."

"Well, I think she must have been a witch," Elsie said.

Abby was so angry she wanted to shout at Elsie for her cruelty, but Sir Chadwick took her firmly by the arm. Then he took a speck of Ice Dust from his waistcoat pocket and carefully blew it in Hilda's direction. As Sir Chadwick hurried her out of the store, Abby watched the glowing dot alight on Hilda.

When they were back on the street, a boy selling papers passed them shouting, "Big news. Read all about it. Octopus stolen from Aquarium. Read all about it."

"Let's go to the Pavilion Theater, Abby, I want to rehearse my new melodrama for tonight," said Sir Chadwick. "And the Atlantis Boat must have arrived by now. The others will be looking for us."

"What about Wolfbane?" asked Abby.

Sir Chadwick shrugged. "He's obviously gone into hiding with Hilda. I'll make the elves search for him."

Sure enough, when they arrived at the crowded pier, the tide was in and they saw the Atlantis Boat tied up to one of the docks.

Spike, Captain Starlight, and the Great Mandini stood on the deck. Abby noticed a sign on a passing pleasure craft. It said:

ARE YOU IN THE PICTURE?
COME TO
WARLOCK'S PHOTOGRAPHIC SHOP
IN THE HIGH STREET AND
SEE FOR YOURSELF

A man was taking a picture of the pier with an enormous camera. Even at a distance, the photographer looked to Abby very much like all of the men she had met at the Ministry of Time.

Sir Chadwick hailed the crew of the Atlantis Boat as they scrambled up a ladder and climbed over the railings onto the pier.

"It was fantastic traveling through time, Abby," said Spike. "It really took my breath away."

"It did mine, too," said Abby. Then Spike noticed how tanned she was. "Gosh, you're brown."

"We've been here for ages. There's been a heat wave," Abby explained. "Sir Chadwick and I have been appearing on the stage!"

Sir Chadwick escorted them inside the empty Pavilion Theater, and they looked about in admiration.

"A handsome venue in which to perform," said Mandini.

"It is excellent," agreed Sir Chadwick. He pointed to the long windows on each side of the auditorium. "And not so stuffy as a regular theater on a hot night. They can keep those windows open, so we get a sea breeze."

Mandini nodded. "How refreshing. Many are the evenings I've been stifled by the heat of the limelights."

Sir Chadwick sat down with them in the stalls and told them what had happened since they had last been together.

"So you see," he said finally, "coincidence piles upon coincidence. I think I must make a quick trip to London tomorrow on the fourteenth and demand to see the records at the Ministry of Coincidence."

"Can you do that?" asked Spike.

"In certain circumstances, appeals are possible," Sir Chadwick replied. "And I'm sure those blasted Wizards altered my watch so we couldn't intercept Wolfbane. It's kept perfect time for the past hundred years."

Captain Starlight wasn't convinced. "Won't making an appeal complicate things even further?" he said. "Surely we should just concentrate on getting Hilda back and returning to our own time."

Sir Chadwick shook his head. "Things are already vastly complicated." Then he slapped his head. "Good heavens! What a fool I've been. I think I begin to see now what this is all about."

"Tell us," said the Great Mandini. "I'm aching to know."

Sir Chadwick waved to Abby. "The night after tomorrow, June 15, a great storm is due. It will blow away the pier and cause great loss of life. Is that correct?"

"Correct," said Abby.

"But according to Mary Bowsprit's diary, Jack Elvin is due to meet her father on June 17, so that Josiah can take him back to Speller, am I still correct?"

"Correct," repeated Abby.

"Then there is a time paradox," said Sir Chadwick.

"What's a paradox?" asked Spike.

"I'm still trying to work it out," said Abby.

"A paradox is a sort of contradiction," said Sir Chadwick quickly. "I'll try to explain it again. The pier, with this theater, is due to be destroyed on June 15, isn't it?"

They all nodded and Sir Chadwick continued. "So Jack Elvin is due to be killed in the disaster, but he isn't, because we know he meets Josiah Bowsprit on the seventeenth."

"Unless Wolfbane manages to alter events completely," Captain Starlight pointed out grimly. "Then the future won't exist as we know it."

"Correct," said Sir Chadwick. "But now I begin to think this is really all about Jack Elvin, not Hilda. She was just the means Wolfbane used to lure us back into the past."

"I see," said Captain Starlight. "And now, Wolfbane will have you and Abby and Jack Elvin on the stage on the night of the storm. That way he can wipe you three out of history."

"You're right," said Sir Chadwick. "I really must go up to London tomorrow and appeal to the Ministry."

"Why not go right away?" said Abby.

Sir Chadwick shook his head. "There's something important I must do here in Torgate tonight."

High up in the shadows among the wooden rafters of the theater, something stirred.

It was Baal, the great spider, listening to every word.

24

Abby and Spike Receive a Surprise

That afternoon, Captain Starlight, Spike, and Mandini carried out an investigation. First, they examined the superstructure of the Pavilion Theater, and then they toured all the underwater parts of the pier in the Atlantis Boat. What they found was worrisome.

"Wolfbane must have worked fast," Mandini said grimly. "All the underwater supports have been eaten through. It looks as though he has used some sort of acid."

"And the theater is unsafe, too," said Spike. He slapped one of the steel pillars that supported it. "They've used acid on these as well."

"So a storm would easily blow it over," said Starlight.

"Can we repair it without anyone noticing?" asked Sir Chadwick.

"Easily, with the tools we have aboard the Atlantis Boat," said Starlight.

"Do we have any Ice Dust aboard the boat?" asked Sir Chadwick. "My supply is pretty limited."

"A chest full," said Mandini. "It was already on board."

"Excellent — but I do wish I knew where Wolfbane was," said Sir Chadwick.

While Captain Starlight and Mandini began to carry out repairs to the pier, Abby asked Sir Chadwick if she could show Spike the town.

"As long as you don't wander off too far," he said. "We may need you."

"We'll stay close," said Abby, and they set off, each with a pocketful of pennies.

First, Abby led Spike to the High Street and Warlock's Photographic Shop. The door was ajar but the premises were deserted and quite bare, but for an envelope lying on the counter. Written on it were the words:

To be collected on behalf of Mr. Jack Elvin.

Inside it was the photograph of the Atlantis Boat with Spike, Captain Starlight, and Mandini aboard that would eventually end up in Mary Bowsprit's album.

"How did you know this would be here?" Spike asked, surprised.

Abby shrugged. "I didn't, really, but I think I'm getting to know the way the Wizards do things."

"How's that?" asked Spike.

"It's almost as if we're a game to them. Like pieces on a board. They move us about without telling us why and see how we react to situations. Look how we got here weeks early. Then we found Sir Chadwick's watch was wrong."

She passed the envelope to Spike. "Better give that to Jack Elvin when you see him."

"Where to now?" asked Spike, pocketing the envelope.

"Let's have some fun," said Abby, and they headed for the fair.

They went on all the rides except the carousel, which still

had an OUT OF ORDER sign on it, and they didn't enter the haunted house that, for some reason, neither of them much fancied.

Finally, they were buying ice creams from a man with a cart on the promenade when, suddenly, Abby stopped and clutched Spike's arm.

"It's Wolfbane," she whispered.

Spike looked up to see a familiar figure striding toward them. It was Wolfbane, accompanied by Mr. Entwhistle, the detective.

It was too late for them to run away. Abby and Spike just stood frozen with fear.

But the hateful figure looked straight at them as he approached and gave no sign of recognition. The detective nodded curtly to Abby as they passed.

Wolfbane was wearing a black top hat and frock coat. He carried a Gladstone bag and brandished a large silver-topped walking stick. Abby just had time to see the name *Sir Morden Hardcastle* embossed on the bag in gold letters. The two men crossed the road and entered the Darkwood Arms.

Spike and Abby ran back to the theater and found Sir Chadwick. He was rehearsing his one-act melodrama and was dressed in the wig, false nose, and beard he wore as the drunken father.

"Sir Chadwick," Abby said breathlessly. "We've just seen Wolfbane on the promenade with the detective."

"Are you sure?" said Sir Chadwick.

"Well, it looked just like him," said Spike, "but he didn't recognize Abby and me. He had a big stick and a bag with 'Sir Morden Hardcastle' written on the side."

Sir Chadwick shook his head. "So, Sir Morden Hardcastle,

the man who hunts Jack Elvin, looks exactly like Wolfbane. Yet another coincidence," he said. "Where did they go?"

"Into the Darkwood Arms."

Just then, the seven elves arrived. "Jack will be along in a minute," said Lupin.

Sir Chadwick studied the elves for a moment. "Lupin," he said, "would you know the difference between a changeling and a Night Witch?"

"Of course I would. Why?" Lupin answered, puzzled.

"I want you to do something that might be dangerous. Are you up for it?"

"I'm your elf," said Lupin stoutly.

A few minutes later, two curious figures hurried along the pier toward the Darkwood Arms. Sir Chadwick, still in his drunken father makeup and costume, was linked arm in arm with a very thin figure in a long overcoat and a large beard.

The top half of the bearded figure was Lupin. He was standing on the shoulders of Spike, who was concealed beneath the long overcoat.

They entered the Darkwood Arms, and Sir Chadwick looked about him in the gloomy interior. A few drinkers stood at the bar. Cecil Entwhistle, the detective, and his companion sat at a table under an engraved mirror.

Sir Morden Hardcastle looked so like Wolfbane it took Sir Chadwick by surprise. "It *must* be Wolfbane," he muttered as he bought himself a glass of beer and a lemonade for Lupin.

"Who am I supposed to be checking?" asked Lupin.

"The man wearing the top hat. He's over there, under the mirror," hissed Sir Chadwick.

"Great toadstools and oak leaves!" whispered Lupin in horror. "It *is* Sir Morden Hardcastle."

"Are you sure?" said Sir Chadwick.

"Positive," said Lupin.

"That's all I wanted to know," said Sir Chadwick. "Drink up." They hurried back to the theater and called the others together.

"Coincidence on coincidence on coincidence," began Sir Chadwick. "It seems to me that Sir Morden Hardcastle must be Wolfbane's changeling brother."

"Are you sure?" asked Mandini.

"There can't be any other explanation," said Sir Chadwick. "Wolfbane's parents must have exchanged another of their sons for a human child."

"What happened to the human babies that the Night Witches took, Sir Chadwick?" asked Abby.

"The Night Witches used to bring them up as their slaves, Abby," Sir Chadwick said.

"Who put a stop to it?" asked Spike.

"The Light Witches," said Sir Chadwick.

"He's being rather modest, Abby," said Mandini. "It was a glorious episode in the history of the Light Witches. And Sir Chadwick led our army. That's why he became Grand Master."

"I thought you'd always been an actor, Sir Chadwick," said Abby.

Mandini shook his head. "If you're a Light Witch, you can't be an actor all the time, Abby," he said. "You know how long we live. People would notice that Sir Chadwick Street had been a star for hundreds of years. So every sixty years or so, we in the theatrical profession retire for a while. In the meantime, we have to do something else. In his last retirement, Sir Chadwick took up soldiering."

"I see," said Abby. "So, I wonder what happened to the child who was replaced by Sir Morden Hardcastle."

"It will be in the records at the Ministry of Coincidence," said Sir Chadwick. Perhaps we'll look tomorrow — if we have time."

"Am I coming with you to London?" asked Abby.

Sir Chadwick nodded. "I think it's best if you stay close to me for the time being."

"Will we go in the Atlantis Boat?"

"I think not," replied Sir Chadwick. "Captain Starlight and Mandini may need her. We'll take the train." Then he appealed to Mandini. "Would you mind filling our place on the bill at the theater tomorrow? We might be back late."

"Delighted to be of service," Mandini replied.

High above them, Baal the Spider stirred in the shadows.

25

Well Met by Moonlight

That evening, Spike, Mandini, and Captain Starlight sat in the front row of the orchestra at the Pavilion Theater and watched Abby and Sir Chadwick's performance.

First on the bill was their song-and-dance routine. Later on, they performed the one-act play Sir Chadwick had written, *Saving a Drunken Father*. Afterward the three guests came backstage to offer their congratulations.

"You were very good, Abby," said Spike. "I really liked the part when you broke Sir Chadwick's gin bottle."

"Thank you, Spike," Abby said graciously. "But it was really Sir Chadwick who did everything. I just opened my mouth and his words came tumbling out."

"Nonsense, child," said Sir Chadwick, who had put his head in Abby's dressing-room door. He was still wearing his heavy makeup, wig, and false nose. "You're an absolute natural. I can always spot talent."

Just then, Iron Fist Jones tapped him on the shoulder. "I've given Captain Starlight and Mr. Mandini a glass of champagne in your dressing room, sir, as you instructed. But there's a young lady waiting at the stage door who wants to see you. Should I tell her to go away?"

"No, thank you, Iron Fist," said Sir Chadwick. "I've been expecting her."

"Will you want to take off your costume and makeup first, sir?"

"No," he replied. "I'll see her just as I am."

Sir Chadwick made his way to the stage door, and, as he'd expected, found the first Hilda Bluebell waiting. The pier was deserted now since all of the theatergoers had returned to the town. The sea shone like silver in the moonlight.

Hilda looked shy and a little embarrassed. "Mr. Stanhope," she said quickly. "It's really very kind of you to see me, but I felt I had to speak to you. It was as if something compelled me to come here."

"That's quite all right, my dear," Sir Chadwick answered with a smile, remembering the speck of Ice Dust he had blown in her direction in the clothing store that morning.

Less nervous now, Hilda continued. "It's just that I want to go on the stage more than anything in the world and I wondered if you had any advice for me."

Sir Chadwick studied her for a moment. She really did look very beautiful in the moonlight. He wanted to take her in his arms, but instead he took out a notebook and scribbled a message. Then, without Hilda seeing, he put it into an envelope with a speck of Ice Dust.

"Go to London tomorrow," he instructed. "And give this to Mr. Michael Dillon, the manager of the Alhambra Theater in Shaftesbury Avenue. He's a very good friend of mine and he will give you a job in the company."

Hilda looked at the envelope and then at Sir Chadwick. She was so overcome she couldn't speak.

"It's very hard work in the theater, you know," he said gently.

"I don't mind," said Hilda, suddenly finding her voice. "I'll work and I'll work. It's what I want to do more than anything else in life." But then another thought occurred to her, and she looked fleetingly worried.

Sir Chadwick saw the look and instantly guessed what was going through her mind. "You don't have enough money to go to London, do you?" he asked.

Hilda now looked confused. "Perhaps I'll be able to borrow it. I'll get there somehow."

Sir Chadwick reached into his pocket and produced a five-pound banknote. "Take this so you can buy some lunch and afford a hotel room."

"But I can't, you've been so kind already . . ." Her voice trailed away.

Sir Chadwick shook his head. "You can pay me back in the future." He patted her arm. "Good night, Hilda, and good luck."

She took a few steps and then turned. "How did you know my name?" she asked.

"It was just a guess," Sir Chadwick called after her. "You look just like a Hilda I used to know."

She turned away with a happy smile, and he watched as she walked away in the moonlight.

26

Hilda Learns of Wolfbane's Plans

The Hilda kidnapped by Wolfbane became aware of a dreadful smell. This told her at once that she was among Night Witches. Wolfbane had given her a strong sleeping potion, and she had been unconscious since he had snatched her away.

As she began to revive, all she could remember was Wolfbane's face leering at her from the spectral carriage, then blackness. She could feel her eyes were blindfolded and her hands and feet tied to a chair.

Some people in her predicament would have panicked, but Hilda was too angry. Instead of struggling, she forced herself to keep still.

If the Night Witches were going to have killed her, she reasoned, they would have done so immediately. They must have taken her captive for some other reason. That meant there was time, and in that time anything could happen.

She was very hungry and thirsty, so she judged she must have been unconscious for ages. Yet she felt strangely hopeful.

All Light Witches could perform magic, but beyond that they each had different abilities. Hilda could communicate with the birds. She let her thoughts go out and she knew there was a force of goodness close to her.

After a few minutes, she heard a tapping sound then something falling to the ground. She felt a tugging on her blindfold. It came away, and she saw two barn owls sitting on a table in front of her.

"Thank you, friends," she said, and the owls hooted a greeting.

Hilda blinked. She was in a large cellar, dimly lit by candlelight. High in the wall was an opening through which the owls had entered. The grill they had knocked aside lay on the floor.

"Where am I?" Hilda asked them.

"You're in Torgate," answered an owl.

"Torgate! I used to live here." She looked down at her clothes. "I wonder why I'm dressed like this. Do you know the date?"

"I'm not sure of the exact day," said an owl. "But the year is 1894."

"Thank you," Hilda said. "Now, will you undo these ropes, please?"

But before the owls could act, there was the sound of people approaching.

"Hide," said Hilda, and the owls quickly flew out.

The door swung open, and Wolfbane entered with Lucia and Caspar.

"Did you hear a flapping sound, Mother?" Wolfbane said to Lucia, then he saw Hilda's blindfold on the floor.

"Ah, Miss Bluebell, you are awake," Wolfbane said. "And your blindfold has come undone. Never mind."

Hilda looked at the pair with contempt. "Sir Chadwick will hunt you down for this outrage, Wolfbane," she said defiantly.

"Do you think so?" Wolfbane answered mildly. "I do hope you're right. I'm looking forward to meeting him. Mind you, he hasn't been very successful so far, has he?"

"Why don't we kill her now?" said Lucia Cheeseman. Caspar the Raven hopped up and down eagerly on her shoulder.

"And spoil all the fun?" answered her son. "I think not. I want her alive for the fate I have in store for her." He turned away, saying, "Baal should be here any moment. I'm anxious to hear his report."

A scrabbling sound came from the corner of the cellar where there was a large hole in the wall. Suddenly, a gigantic spider scuttled across the room and stood at Wolfbane's feet.

"Ah, Baal," Wolfbane said, reaching down to tickle the monster. "And what have you to tell me about Sir Chadwick's plans?"

The creature began to talk in a strange hissing voice. "I hid in the theater, as you instructed, Great One. They have repaired the damage to the pier."

"I thought they would," nodded Wolfbane. "Continue."

"Sir Chadwick is very suspicious of all the coincidences. He is going to London with the child, Abby Clover. He plans to visit the Ministry of Coincidence and appeal to the Wizards for more information."

"Excellent," said Wolfbane. "I think I'll dispose of him in London — and the child Abby Clover. Then we can take care of Jack Elvin and his vile little elves at our leisure."

"Do be careful, my son," said Lucia. "Wizards can be very tricky to deal with."

"What do I care for Wizards now I have the secret of time

travel?" he answered scornfully. "By the way, how is the latest batch of Bigger Powder coming along?"

"Almost ready," replied Lucia.

He looked to Hilda. "My mother and I have to go now, Miss Bluebell. But we shall leave Baal to keep you company." He looked down at the spider. "You can hurt her, Baal, but don't eat her. I want her alive, remember."

Wolfbane and his mother departed, and Hilda studied the horrible creature. Baal crouched down, and she could see his great hairy body pulsating as he breathed. Then, with two clawlike jaws opening and shutting, he began to approach her.

When the giant spider was only inches away, there was a sudden beating of wings and the owls reappeared, accompanied by two fearsome-looking hawks. Baal took one look at the predatory birds and scuttled away to hide in his hole.

"Thank you, friends," said Hilda. "Now, will you please undo these ropes?"

The hawks made short work of the knots and before long Hilda was massaging her wrists. She climbed the cellar stairs and found herself in a pharmacy. Accompanied by the owls, she let herself out onto a street that was glowing in the gaslight.

"I know where I am," said Hilda, looking about her. "This is Torgate Promenade." What should I do, she wondered. Then she remembered Baal's words. Sir Chadwick and Abby were going to London to the Ministry of Coincidence. So they must have followed her into the past! A clock nearby chimed the hour. Eleven o'clock. Time to catch the midnight train. I'll go to London and first thing in the morning I'll ask about Chadwick and Abby at the Ministry of Coincidence, she decided. I must warn them both that Wolfbane intends to trap them.

Then she remembered that she had no money. The hawks had gone, but the owls still hovered near.

"Do you know where I can get some money?" Hilda asked.

The first owl shook its head, but the second said, "I know a magpie that has three gold sovereigns in its nest." It flew off and soon reappeared with the coins.

"I will always be grateful," said Hilda.

"You're most welcome, my dear," said the second owl, and the two birds flew off into the night.

With her mind made up, Hilda turned toward the station. She barely missed seeing a younger and much happier version of herself, who had just left Sir Chadwick at the door of the Pavilion Theater, walking away from the pier.

27

Frustration at the Ministry of Coincidence

Abby was excited the following morning. It would be the first time she had ever traveled on a train. Sir Chadwick bought return tickets to Waterloo station and then took her to the head of the platform to see the steam engine that would take them to London.

The great green-and-black machine huffed and hissed and impressed her no end. The conductor gave her a cheery wave.

After they had taken their seats, the train pulled out of Torgate and quite soon entered a long tunnel that emerged at the edge of Darkwood Forest. They passed Speller station and the level crossing.

"How long will the journey take now, Sir Chadwick?" asked Abby as they pulled away from Speller.

"Not much more than an hour," he replied without looking up from his newspaper. He was reading the latest account of the octopus that was missing from Torgate Aquarium.

Abby looked out of the window during the whole journey through the pretty rolling countryside, occasionally interrupted by a village or town.

Eventually, Sir Chadwick commented that they had reached the outskirts of London, and Abby thought the journey must soon be over. But the train continued through seemingly endless miles of closely packed houses, parks, municipal buildings, and factories. She was astonished that it was so big.

"Waterloo is a long way off yet," said Sir Chadwick. "These are just the suburbs."

At last, they pulled into their destination, and Abby was openmouthed at the sight of the bustling crowds as they crossed the station concourse. There were more people under the great glass roof than in the whole of Speller.

Porters pushed carts loaded with luggage, followed by ladies and gentlemen in fine clothes. Others in the crowd carried their own bags as they made their way through the busy throng. Everyone seemed to be in such a hurry, and all were going in different directions. Abby thought they must all be late for urgent appointments.

She was so interested in looking about her that she bumped into a soldier in a scarlet coat and pillbox hat. He saluted her and laughed as she gazed up at him in admiration.

Once outside, Sir Chadwick managed to find a hansom cab. Soon they were trotting through the cobbled streets toward Trafalgar Square.

When Sir Chadwick had paid for the cab, Abby began to make for the statue of Charles I, but Sir Chadwick held out a restraining hand. "We don't have an appointment yet, Abby. Follow me."

He led her to the base of Nelson's Column and stood before one of the huge lion statues. When there was no one about, he addressed the lion, saying, "My name is Sir Chadwick Street, I wish to have a meeting with the Permanent Undersecretary to the Minister of Coincidence."

To Abby's surprise, the lion blinked twice and said in a low rumbling voice, "And what is your business?"

"I demand an immediate Court of Inquiry into the events taking place at Torgate."

The lion blinked again and said, "Take the west fountain entrance."

"Thank you," said Sir Chadwick, ushering Abby toward the fountain indicated.

When they stood in front of it, Sir Chadwick said, "Do exactly as I do." He held his nose, jumped into the water and vanished from sight.

"Oh, well," said Abby and, holding her own nose, she jumped in after him. A moment later, she found herself, quite dry, standing at the top of Whitehall next to Sir Chadwick. The Wizard World looked exactly the same as it had on her last visit. Snow was still falling but she and Sir Chadwick were not wearing their coats.

"It's a bit chilly," said Sir Chadwick. "But if we walk quickly we'll stay warm."

They hurried down Whitehall, heads bent forward against the flurry of snow. This time, Sir Chadwick stopped in front of a different building. It was just as imposing as the Ministry of Time, and it seemed to have the same doorman.

"Haven't we met before?" Abby asked him.

"I do hope so," said the tall, thin man. "This is the Ministry of Coincidence. We've been expecting you. Follow the same directions as when you last visited."

Once again, they entered a cavernous lobby lined with

statues and climbed a vast staircase to trudge along an endless corridor.

When they reached another bust of Merlin, Sir Chadwick knocked on the door next to it.

"Come," shouted a voice.

When they entered, Abby was surprised to find that instead of the crowded little room she had expected, this office was huge. There was a massive desk that stretched the entire length of the mighty room and sitting at the end was a figure looking exactly like the Undersecretary at the Ministry of Time. He had a thick file open before him.

"Sit down," the man instructed.

Abby and Sir Chadwick took the two chairs that were nearest to them. Abby could hardly see the undersecretary, he was so far away.

"Let us begin," he said, and banged on the table with a gavel. "This is a Court of Inquiry brought about at the request of Sir Chadwick Street, Grand Master of the Ancient Order of Light Witches. Make your submission, Sir Chadwick. And please be brief, I have a very busy day ahead of me."

Sir Chadwick cleared his throat. "Miss Clover and I are visiting 1894 by permission of the Ministry of Time —" he began.

"Yes, yes, I know that," said the undersecretary impatiently. "Please get to the point."

"We came here with the express purpose of apprehending Wolfbane, Master of the Night Witches, who has broken the Wizards' Treaty governing time travel."

"Yes, yes, I know that, too."

Sir Chadwick cleared his throat again. "I submit that we are being hampered in the pursuit of our task by ministerial interference. I demand that we should be allowed to finish our business as we see fit. Or be given some explanation as to why the Wizards are manipulating events in such a mysterious fashion."

"Request denied," said the undersecretary briskly and he banged his gavel. "That will be all. This Court of Inquiry is over."

"This is disgraceful," shouted Sir Chadwick angrily. "I demand some sort of explanation for the behavior of the Ministry."

The undersecretary looked up. "I told you this inquiry is over," he said. "You're the second person who has come here today demanding action from us. The last person who called was . . ." He glanced down at his file. "Miss Hilda Bluebell. She wanted to know where Sir Chadwick Street and Abby Clover were. I had to tell her that I had no idea and send her on her way."

"But I am Sir Chadwick Street and this is Abby Clover," Sir Chadwick shouted.

"Well, I had no inkling you were coming when she was here earlier, did I?" said the man in a suddenly reasonable voice.

"This is impossible," said Sir Chadwick. He took Abby's hand. "We might as well go."

"Quite so. If that's all," said the undersecretary.

Sir Chadwick was about to leave when he paused. "There is one thing."

"Yes."

"After the War of the Slaves between the Night and the Light Witches, what happened to the babies that were liberated?"

The thin man scratched his head. "I understand some were

assigned new homes, others returned to their parents. It all depended on the circumstances of each particular case."

"I want to trace a child taken from parents called Hardcastle. A changeling was left in the child's place," said Sir Chadwick.

"The doorman will have the answer for you on your way out. Good evening."

"Don't you mean good morning?" asked Abby.

"It's been a very long day," said the undersecretary, lowering his head.

In the corridor once again, Abby said, "That seemed to be a waste of time."

"Not entirely," said Sir Chadwick. "At least we know that Hilda has escaped from Wolfbane, although heaven knows how."

"True," said Abby. "But we still don't know where she is."

"Eventually, Hilda will head for the Alhambra Theater. That's standard Light Witch procedure in time of trouble," Sir Chadwick said confidently as they descended the staircase.

As they approached the doorman, he held out an envelope. Sir Chadwick took it from him and was about to open it as they walked out into the snow, but the doorman shouted after them, "Trafalgar Square exit has just been closed for maintenance. You'll have to use the emergency exit."

"Which emergency exit?" replied Sir Chadwick, stuffing the unopened envelope into his pocket.

"The one that comes out in Regent Street," the doorman replied. "Take care, the time frame is a bit wonky."

"Oh, wonderful!" said Sir Chadwick bitterly. "A nice long walk to Regent Street in this snow. We'd better try and get a cab."

Luckily, a hansom cab came along as he spoke and they

climbed aboard. Abby didn't mind the ride: London in Wizard World looked lovely in the snow, like a Christmas card someone had once sent her aunt Lucy.

"If I remember correctly," said Sir Chadwick as they descended from the cab in Regent Street, "this exit from Wizard World is the street crossing in front of the Café Royal." He paused for a moment and said, "Yes, I'm sure this lamppost is the key."

He pushed part of the decoration at the base of the lamp and, taking Abby by the elbow, began to cross the road. Halfway across, the snow vanished, but it wasn't morning anymore. Instead, it was a fine summer evening.

Abby was surprised by the amount of traffic in Regent Street, and it moved quite fast. Coaches, carts, drays, and hansom cabs rushed past, the horses' hooves and the iron-bound wheels clashing and clattering over the cobblestones.

Sir Chadwick looked about him. "Well, he was right about the time frame being wonky," he said. "It should still be morning. Let's hope it's the same day." He bought an evening newspaper from a vendor who stood outside the Café Royal. "Yes, it's all right," he said after consulting the date.

As he was glancing through the rest of the newspaper, Abby looked back across the street and saw Hilda walking in the direction of Piccadilly Circus. Before she could point her out to Sir Chadwick, an old lady shuffled toward Hilda. She had a small dog on a lead. Suddenly, there was a gap in the traffic and the little dog broke away from the old lady and ran into the road.

Without hesitation, Hilda dashed after the dog. But a great black carriage pulled by massive plumed horses appeared and thundered toward Hilda.

Hilda bent down to scoop up the little dog. As she did so, it turned into Caspar, Lucia Cheeseman's raven, and flapped away.

Hilda looked up, helplessly, to see the black horses and the spectral carriage descending upon her. Wolfbane and Lucia sat on the driver's bench, each of their faces a mask of hatred. Without stopping to think, Abby performed her tobbing trick. She vanished from her place next to Sir Chadwick and instantly reappeared beside Hilda.

Abby held up a hand to the horses that were bearing down on them and shouted, *"Won nruter!"* She had no idea where the words had come from.

The horses reared up, and the flesh seemed to dissolve from their bones. Wolfbane and Lucia screamed in frustration. Instantly, Sir Chadwick stood over Abby and Hilda, wand drawn, but the skeletal horses had vanished, along with the carriage and its vicious passengers.

"Abby! Chadwick, darling," Hilda cried with relief. "Thank heavens I've found you."

Sir Chadwick took both their arms and ushered them across the road and into the Café Royal.

They entered a large smoke-filled room, furnished with potted plants and marble-topped tables where people sat drinking and smoking while waiters in long white aprons moved among them. A hubbub of many conversations filled the crowded room.

They took a table and a waiter came instantly to take their order.

"Two large brandies and a cup of hot chocolate, please, Burlington," Sir Chadwick said without thinking.

"Certainly, Mr. Courtney," the waiter answered and hurried away.

"Why did he call you Mr. Courtney?" asked Abby.

"Did he?" said Sir Chadwick. "He must think I'm me."

Abby looked confused and Hilda smiled. "I think Sir Chadwick has the name Roland Courtney in this time, Abby."

"Oh, yes, the Great Mandini explained all that to me. But why are you still called Hilda Bluebell?"

"I don't become well known for at least another hundred years or so, so there was no need to change my name," she said, squeezing Sir Chadwick's arm. "Although I must say all this time travel can get confusing!"

The glasses of brandy and Abby's chocolate arrived, and after taking a sip, Sir Chadwick looked at Abby. "Who taught you to do what you did when the carriage was about to run Hilda down?" he asked, puzzled.

Abby looked confused. "You mean tobbing? You did, Sir Chadwick, don't you remember?"

Sir Chadwick shook his head. "No, I don't mean tobbing, Abby. I mean, who taught you the words you shouted when you made the spectral horses rear up?"

Abby shrugged. "No one taught me, I just made them up. I don't think they mean anything at all."

Sir Chadwick shook his head. "On the contrary, they were part of an anagram spell."

"What's that?" asked Abby.

"A very advanced and very powerful type of magic. Only some Light Witches learn to do it when they're very old. Even I can't do them yet."

"What? Make up anagrams?"

"No, use anagrams to do magic without Ice Dust. The words you shouted were *Won nruter.* If you rearrange the letters you get *return now*, and that's what happened to the spectral carriage. It returned to the nether regions."

"Will Wolfbane and his mother get out again?"

"I expect so," said Sir Chadwick.

"Well, I'm glad it worked," said Abby. "Even if it is only temporary."

"So am I," said Hilda, squeezing Sir Chadwick's hand again.

"Just a moment," he said. "There's something I must do before anything else."

He drew his wand and pointed it at Hilda. The tip quivered for a moment and then dipped to point at a button on her coat. Carefully, Sir Chadwick took a pinch of Ice Dust from his pocket and placed it on the marble tabletop. Then he took a small silver pocketknife from his waistcoat and, with a sudden deft movement, cut off the button on Hilda's coat and dropped it on the Ice Dust on the table.

They all watched as the button slowly turned into a very large beetle that wriggled for a moment and then vanished.

"A spy of Wolfbane's," said Sir Chadwick. "That creature was to tell him where you were. He must have guessed you'd escape and find us. Incidentally, how did you escape?"

Hilda told them of her rescue by the owls. "I must have been unconscious for ages," she said, "but I've no idea for how long."

"Well, here's a fine gathering!" said a familiar voice, and there was Paddy the Pooka standing before them. He was in his human form, wearing a pale-gray frock coat and top hat, and had a green carnation in his buttonhole.

28

Sir Chadwick Admires
a Performance

Paddy, my dear boy," said Sir Chadwick. This time he sounded more enthusiastic about the pooka's unexpected appearance. "What brings you to town?"

"Just catching up with a few friends while I've got the time," Paddy the Pooka replied, reaching into his waistcoat pocket. "Will you accept a little present from me to round off the day?" He placed three theater tickets on the table before them. "They're for a sold-out performance," said Paddy. Then with a wink he added, "But I've got influence. Michael Dillon, the manager, is a pal of mine."

"Will you join us for a drink?" suggested Sir Chadwick, but Paddy had already disappeared.

Hilda picked up the tickets and looked at the date. "What a coincidence," she said. "Do you know what the date is?"

Abby and Sir Chadwick looked up. "It's the day I got my job at the Alhambra Theater." She reached out and squeezed Sir Chadwick's hand affectionately. "And the first night of your famous performance of *King Lear*, Chadwick. Can we go?"

Sir Chadwick was undecided. "It is a bit of a risk, you know."

"Why?" asked Abby.

Sir Chadwick held up a hand. "Wizard rules of time travel, we're supposed to avoid all contact with our previous selves. It could cause complications."

"I would have thought things are complicated already," said Abby with feeling.

Sir Chadwick relented. "Well, I have never seen myself actually perform. Let's risk it. We can catch the late train back to Torgate."

An hour later, Abby, Hilda, and Sir Chadwick huddled in a doorway in the narrow alley next to the Alhambra Theater in Shaftesbury Avenue.

Sir Chadwick was studying the second hand of his watch. "You should appear any second now, Hilda," he said, and they drew even farther back into the shadows. A figure passed them, and Abby, Hilda, and Sir Chadwick peered out from the doorway.

They could see the younger Hilda walking toward the stage door of the Alhambra Theater, where a man with silver hair and beard stood in the alleyway, smoking a small cigar in the warm evening air.

They watched as the young Hilda handed him a note, which he read, and then ushered her into the theater. As Mr. Dillon entered the theater he dropped the note. A sudden breeze blew the sheet of paper toward Abby.

She caught it and read the contents.

Dear Michael,
Please be so kind as to employ this young lady in the company.
Then forget that she was hired on my instructions.
Yours ever,
Roland Courtney

The Time Witches

Sir Chadwick took the note from her with a smile and tucked it into his pocket. "A touching scene," he said. "A little bit of the history of the theater being made."

A few minutes later, they were seated in the stalls and the curtain rose.

Later, on the train back to Torgate, Hilda said, and not for the first time, "I thought you were absolutely wonderful, Chadwick, quite wonderful, a truly magnificent performance."

He smiled and patted her hand. "I wasn't a bad King Lear, was I?"

"The finest I have ever seen, my love."

"I'm sorry I fell asleep," said Abby.

"It's not really a play for one of your tender years," said Sir Chadwick. "But yes, I do think I played the part adequately."

"I woke up when you were crying at your own performance," said Abby.

"No, no," protested Sir Chadwick. "I had a mote of dust in my eye." He smiled at Hilda. "And you were wonderful, too, dearest."

"I didn't know you were in it, Hilda," said Abby. "I would have tried to stay awake."

"They let me work the thunder machine in the storm," said Hilda.

"Your timing was perfect," said Sir Chadwick.

"Yes, it woke me up," said Abby.

The train passed through the tunnel just before Torgate and, when Sir Chadwick was searching for the tickets, he found the envelope handed to him by the doorman.

"I forgot all about this," he said, taking out a dusty sheet of paper.

"What's that, Chadwick?" asked Hilda.

"Actually, it's about you, dearest. It's a file from the Ministry of Coincidence," he said, studying the document.

After a time he exclaimed, "This information is truly astonishing!" He began to read aloud.

"This is to certify that the child taken from Sir David and Lady Hardcastle was found in the home of Uric and Lucia Cheeseman in Darkwood Forest.

"Mr. and Mrs. Cheeseman denied they were Night Witches, claiming that their own son, Snivel Cheeseman, was a graduate of Merlin College, Oxford.

"While further inquiries were being made, Uric and Lucia Cheeseman fled, leaving the child abandoned.

"Pending her return to her rightful parents, the child was placed in the temporary care of Daisy and Frederick Bluebell, Light Witches, living in the town of Torgate. As is customary in these cases, it would be expected that her foster parents would begin to nurture Hilda as a Light Witch, even though her birth parents were human beings.

"Before the child could be returned to her birth parents, she and her foster parents were all killed in a fire, which totally destroyed the home of Daisy and Frederick Bluebell.

"Uric and Lucia Cheeseman were always suspected of the crime, but nothing could be proved."

Sir Chadwick scratched his head. "This is peculiar, Hilda. According to the Wizard files, you're supposed to be dead. Do you remember your foster parents?"

"No," said Hilda softly. "I only remember the orphanage."

"But you kept the Bluebell name?"

"It was in this," Hilda said, passing him a gold locket she wore on a slender chain around her neck.

Sir Chadwick opened it and saw the name Hilda Bluebell was engraved inside. He passed it to Abby.

"It's starting to grow very warm," she said, puzzled. Then a voice began to speak from the locket.

"This is Daisy Bluebell, creator of this message. I know the locket must be in the possession of a truly great Light Witch because I have spelled it to work only in the proper hands.

"The child, now known as Hilda Bluebell, is in grave danger. The Night Witches are hunting her. Frederick and I have secretly put her in the protection of Torgate Orphanage because we think the Night Witches have traced her to us.

"Hilda's true parents were Sir David and Lady Hardcastle, who were killed by Uric and Lucia Cheeseman. A changeling has usurped their real child. Protect Hilda, for the Night Witches still wish to destroy her."

"Remarkable," said Sir Chadwick softly. *"A truly great Light Witch!"*

"You must have started it working before you handed it to me, Sir Chadwick," said Abby.

"Perhaps so," he replied thoughtfully, taking the locket again and returning it to Hilda.

"So now I know who I really am," said Hilda. "It's a strange feeling after all these years. So Morden Hardcastle was a changeling, deceiving my birth parents with magic, and Wolfbane is Snivel Cheeseman, his brother!"

The train pulled into Torgate station with a hissing sigh.

29

Sir Morden Meets
a Curious Stranger

Sir Morden Hardcastle, wearing white tie and tails, and smoking a large and expensive cigar, sat by a window in the dining room of the Metropole Hotel, drinking champagne. Next to him sat Entwhistle the detective, drinking a pot of ale.

"I'm deeply sorry, sir, but the trail has gone cold," Entwhistle said. "It led here to Torgate, Sir Morden, but I haven't seen hide nor hair of Jack Elvin. I've tried everything. Employed all my skills, but to no avail."

Sir Morden flicked the ash of his cigar in Entwhistle's direction. "You blundering fool, you couldn't find a pimple on the end of your nose."

"That's not fair, sir," protested the detective. "Didn't I track down that widow who owed you back rent? Even though she'd changed her name and was living in the poorhouse, we still got her put in jail."

Sir Morden's face took on a sneering expression. "You have been useful, but you're worn out now. Like an old horse, you should go to the glue factory. Get out of my sight, you're fired."

Entwhistle rose to his feet, swaying and trying to look dignified. "If you're going to take that attitude, I resign. You'll get my bill in the morning."

"Just clear off," Morden snarled. As he watched the detective totter away, he muttered, "I'd give anything to get hold of that swine, Elvin."

There was a sudden fluttering sound, and Sir Morden saw a strange little figure now sitting in the seat Entwhistle had vacated.

The man before him wore a silk top hat and an opera cloak that enveloped the rest of his body. A sharp beaky nose accentuated his features and, beneath the brim of his opera hat, he had little yellow eyes.

"Who the devil are you?" said Sir Morden irritably. "I didn't invite you to join me."

The little man smiled and spoke in a curious croaky voice. "Oh, but you did, I was sitting at the next table and I heard you mention the name Jack Elvin."

"You know where he is?" Morden said, leaning toward the man.

"Let's say I can put you in touch with certain people who could reveal that information."

"Who are they? How do I meet them?"

"You said you'd give anything."

"So how much do you want?" asked Sir Morden contemptuously.

The little man cocked his head to one side. "Just pay my bill."

Sir Morden snapped his fingers to a passing waiter and said, "What does this man owe? I'll pay it."

The waiter returned immediately and handed Sir Morden a bill.

"Five pheasants and an entire Stilton cheese!" he read out in surprise.

"They were delicious," said the little man contentedly.

Sir Morden placed a five-pound note on the plate and turned to his companion. "You say these people really know where Jack Elvin is?"

"They will be able to tell you," said the little man confidently.

"I suppose it's worth a try," said Sir Morden. "Where can I find them?"

"Go to the haunted house in the fair."

"Now?" said Sir Morden impatiently. "The fair is closed, it's nearly midnight."

"What better time to visit a haunted house?" said the little man. "Now, I must be going." He slipped from the chair and walked from the dining room with a strange loping motion.

Sir Morden looked from the window to catch another glimpse of the man, but all he saw was a raven rising into the air.

He did not want to go to the haunted house, but to his surprise found himself leaving the hotel and walking along the promenade. The full moon was reflected in the calm waters of Torgate bay, but he had no interest in the beauty of the scene.

As he had expected, the fair was closed for the night. The flaring gas lamps were extinguished and pipe organs quiet. But he could read the signs on the attractions by the light of the moon.

After some searching, he found the haunted house, and with a shrug tried a door in the side. It opened. He entered a narrow corridor, dimly lit by gaslight. As he walked along it, he heard the muttering sound of voices coming from behind a door.

Morden knocked and a voice called out, "Come in."

As he entered, a dreadful smell made him wrinkle his nose. The room was dimly lit by a single candle. Two figures sat at a table eating from bowls.

A smartly dressed woman looked up and gasped with open-mouthed astonishment.

The man, who sat with his back toward Morden, swiveled around. It was Sir Morden's turn to be surprised. He staggered back, aghast.

The figure that looked up at him could have been his own reflection in a looking glass.

"What trickery is this?" said Wolfbane, glaring angrily at his double.

"I could ask the same," snarled Sir Morden.

The woman rose and looked at him closely. "I think I know who this is, Wolfbane," she said. "I want to introduce your brother, Sir Morden Hardcastle."

"Brother!" both men exclaimed.

"Yes," said Lucia Cheeseman, looking intently at both her sons. "Sit down, the pair of you, and I'll explain."

When Lucia had finished, Sir Morden looked down at the greasy tabletop for a moment. "So that's why I could never bear to be with my parents," he said. Then he nodded to Lucia. "So you are fair people. I must say I've always felt myself to be higher on the social scale than that. At least, the dreadful man who brought me up was a baronet."

"Do you remember the accident they met with when you were quite young?" said Lucia fondly.

Morden shot her a glance. "Their carriage overturned. A wheel came loose somehow."

"Your real father's work. He would be so proud to see you

now," Lucia continued happily. "He always had such high hopes for you."

"Where is my real father?" asked Morden.

"Yes," Wolfbane chimed in. "I've been meaning to ask you that, Mother. I haven't seen him for a hundred or so years."

Lucia waved dismissively. "You know what a dreamer he's always been. He's been on a trip to South America, studying native rituals for as long as I can remember. He'll turn up again one of these days."

"So, what about Jack Elvin?" said Morden impatiently.

"We intend to finish him ourselves," said Wolfbane. "We know exactly where he's going to be in a few days' time. We plan to kill him then."

Morden twisted the head of his walking stick and drew out a wicked-looking sword. "Can't I meet him before that?" he said. "I have my own reasons for wanting him to suffer."

"No," said Wolfbane sharply. "I fully intend to kill him myself."

Lucia sat up and spoke sharply. "Now, Wolfbane," she said. "Don't be greedy. Are you going to deny your only brother this one pleasure?"

Wolfbane shrugged. "Oh, all right," he said reluctantly. "But *I'm* going to kill Abby Clover."

"So where is Jack Elvin now?" asked Sir Morden.

"We don't actually know from moment to moment," said Lucia. "We don't need to if we know where he's going to be at a certain time in the future."

Morden groaned with frustration. "I want to kill him *now*," he snarled.

"I'll see what I can do," said Lucia soothingly. "Can you draw a picture of him?"

The Time Witches

"I'm no artist," said Morden. "But I have a photograph of him here."

"Perfect," said Lucia. "Give it to me."

Morden handed her the picture, and she pointed an index finger in the air and began to write. To Morden's amazement, the name *Jack Elvin* appeared before him, suspended in letters of fire. Lucia held the photograph to the flames, and it burned to ashes.

She took the ashes and blew them into the air. Suddenly, a small figure of Jack Elvin, wearing his new beard and surrounded by elves, appeared dancing in the air before them.

"That's a damned clever trick," said Morden. "How did you do that? Magic, was it?"

Lucia shook her head. "We're Night Witches," she said.

Morden smiled. "Look," he said. "I know you're a pretty low class of person. But there's no need to lie to me. No one is going to know we're related, in any case. Once I've done in that swine Elvin, I'll go back to my estates. We won't be seeing each other again. So there's no need to keep up this pretense about being Night Witches. I can see with my own eyes, you're both just a couple of grubby fakers."

Lucia Cheeseman did not take her eyes from Sir Morden's face. "Wolfbane," she said, "I think it's time you introduced your brother to Baal."

30

A Picnic
in Darkwood Forest

The following day was so hot that Abby decided she didn't want to make her usual visit to the beach.

"Actually, I wouldn't mind a stroll somewhere cool," said Sir Chadwick as he sat with Abby and Hilda in their rooms at the guesthouse. "I've got something I must think about. Suppose we ask Mrs. Greenbower to make us a picnic basket and we go to Darkwood Forest?"

"That would be delightful, Chadwick," said Hilda.

"It may be hot now, but don't forget the great storm is due tonight," said Abby. "The pier is going to be blown away and everybody killed."

Sir Chadwick nodded. "That's what I've got to think about." He sighed. "It's strictly against the Wizards' rules to interfere with the past. But how can we not help the people who are going to be killed in the storm?"

"You have to," said Abby, hunting for her straw hat.

Sir Chadwick stood up. "You're quite right, child," he said firmly. "To blazes with the Wizards' rules. After all, they haven't played straight with us. We'll use all our powers to protect the people on the pier from the storm."

He picked up the telephone and put a speck of Ice Dust in

the receiver. "I'll call the others on the Atlantis Boat and ask them if they wish to go on the picnic." After a moment, Captain Starlight answered his call.

After a brief conversation, Sir Chadwick put down the telephone and said, "Adam and Mandini want to make the pier even stronger. They're going to work on it today. Spike has already gone for a long swim with Benbow, so it's just us three for the picnic in Darkwood Forest."

"How do we get there, Chadwick?" asked Hilda.

"There's a livery stable next to Torgate station," he replied airily. "We'll hire a pony and cart."

A short time later, with Sir Chadwick carrying the picnic basket prepared by Mrs. Greenbower, they made their way to the stable.

To Abby's amusement, the man who ran it looked just like the taxi driver who had driven them to Darkwood Manor. "Everything's out, sir," he said. "Sorry about that."

"You really have nothing left?"

"Well, there's an old donkey cart," said the groom doubtfully. "But the donkey's a bit slow. He's been retired for a few years."

"We're not in a hurry," said Sir Chadwick, and the donkey and cart were produced.

"You'd better get out of the cart and walk when you come to any hills," said the groom as they departed. He slapped the donkey's hide. "This old chap is on his last legs."

"We won't tire him," said Sir Chadwick. "Have no fear."

They set off, and when they came to the first gentle hill on the outskirts of town, Sir Chadwick said, "Everybody out. We'll walk up the hill."

But the donkey said, "Sit tight, Chaddy, darlin'. I could pull you all up twenty of these without turning a hair." It was Paddy the Pooka, and he set off at a brisk trot.

Eventually, he slowed down and led them from the main road along a path into the forest. After a while they came to a shaded grassy hillock, covered with wildflowers. It was on the banks of a stream that flowed over a bed of pebbles.

"Perfect for a picnic," said Hilda as they unhitched Paddy. Mrs. Greenbower's basket was filled with delicious food: ham, cold chicken, fresh bread, cheese, and fruit, but Paddy preferred to crop the grassy bank.

When Sir Chadwick had eaten the last chicken leg, he tilted his straw hat over his eyes and lay back in the deep sweet-smelling grass. Hilda lay beside him.

Paddy whispered to Abby, "Why don't you get up on my back and I'll take you for a ride so we can leave these lovebirds alone for a while?"

Abby did as Paddy suggested, and they set off into the forest. As they rode along, Paddy told her all about his life in Ireland and the magical places his life as a pooka had taken him. Then he suddenly stood quite still.

"What's the matter, Paddy?" Abby asked.

"Shhhh," he said in a whisper. "Be still for a moment and look over there."

Abby followed his gaze. In a sun-drenched clearing in the forest were two unicorns with a foal.

Their white coats gleamed like snow in the bright shafts of sunlight. The three mythical creatures stopped by a small tree, heavy with golden berries. The mare pulled down a branch so that the foal could crop some of the fruit. Then they slowly passed out of sight.

When the unicorns had gone, Paddy entered the clearing.

"Take some of those little berries, Abby," he said. "They're powerful lucky fruit."

Abby took a handful and put them in her pocket, and Paddy walked on. When they finally returned to the riverbank, Sir Chadwick and Hilda were packing up the basket.

"There's no sign of a storm yet, Sir Chadwick," Abby said.

He glanced up at the sky. "And there won't be until Wolfbane gets to work, I think."

"So you think the storm will be Wolfbane making mischief?" said Hilda. "But why, Chadwick?"

He shrugged. "He may have a reason, or he might just be in a nasty mood. But whatever the cause, it's not altogether a bad thing."

"Not a bad thing?" said Hilda, puzzled.

"Yes, my dear. We haven't been able to find Wolfbane's hiding place, despite the efforts made by Adam, Mandini, and the elves. But we know he will come out tonight, and we'll be ready for him."

"Are there enough of us, Chadwick?" Hilda asked.

"I think so," said Sir Chadwick. "I believe he only has the one Night Witch he brought with him in the spectral carriage. We should be strong enough to deal with the two of them. If he wants to destroy the pier, he must be near the theater tonight." He glanced at his watch. "Time to be on our way."

"What a lovely day it's been," said Hilda with a sigh. "I just hope it doesn't end in tragedy."

"Amen to that, darlin'," said Paddy softly as they hitched him to the donkey cart and set off toward Torgate in the last of the glorious sunshine.

31

Sir Chadwick and Wolfbane Make Their Plans

The tourists enjoying the thrills of the haunted house in Torgate fair had no idea what was hidden deep within its structure. In a secret compartment, Wolfbane and his mother were finalizing their plans.

Sir Morden Hardcastle had joined them at the dining table, listening as Wolfbane ran through the events that were to take place that evening.

"You've hired a boat, Mother?" he snapped.

"That was done first thing this morning, dear."

"And the supplies of Bigger Powder are loaded on board?"

"Yes."

Wolfbane addressed his brother. "Jack Elvin and his elves are the last act on the bill tonight. When they've finished and are taking their bow, you can go onto the stage and kill him in front of a packed audience."

Morden stirred petulantly. "Does that mean I'll have to sit through the entire blasted performance? I hate seeing common people enjoying themselves."

Wolfbane sighed. "I really don't care. You have a ticket

booked in the front row of the orchestra. You can take up your position whenever you please."

Morden thought for a moment. "Actually it might be rather pleasant to watch the show, knowing what a finale I have in store for them." Then he thought of something. "Elvin and the elves may recognize me if I'm sitting in the front row."

"Wear a false face," suggested Lucia.

"What's that?" asked Morden.

"I'll show you," said Lucia. She took some rubbery material from her handbag and placed it on the table. "What was the name of that butcher whose face you used?" she asked Wolfbane.

"Button," he answered.

Lucia waved her hands over the rubbery material and chanted:

"Button's face I want to make,
give to me a perfect fake."

The material quivered, then took on the shape of a cheery smiling countenance. Lucia handed it to Morden. "Put this on before you go to the theater."

"Yes," said Morden. "I'll tear it off when I leap onto the stage. That should terrify them."

Wolfbane nodded. "Just remember to leave the theater immediately. There's a large window next to the wings. I suggest you make your exit through that and get off the pier as quickly as you can."

"Morden Hardcastle fears nothing," he snarled. "I want to stay and enjoy the horror of the crowd."

Wolfbane sighed again. "Will you explain it to him,

Mother? He seems to have difficulty understanding my instructions."

Lucia leaned forward and said patiently, "Wolfbane is going to completely destroy the theater, my dear. If you stay, you will be killed with the rest of the audience."

Morden was still not convinced. "What about you two? How is it no harm will come to you?"

Wolfbane slammed a fist down on the table. "Because we're Night Witches, you feather-headed idiot! We can protect ourselves, but we won't have time to look after you as well. So, once you've killed Jack Elvin, get out as quickly as you can."

Morden nodded in a sullen fashion. "I still don't like it," he said. "I was hoping to make him die a slow death."

"One more thing," said Lucia. She handed a small glass vial to Morden. "Just a little added protection."

"How can this protect me?"

"It's Black Dust that I've spelled. If you get into difficulties, swallow it, and any evil wish you have will come true."

Morden had seen enough of Wolfbane's and Lucia's powers by now not to doubt her. He placed the vial in his top pocket.

Wolfbane continued. "Right," he said, "I'm going to go over the plan just once more." As he spoke, they could hear the distant screams of the happy crowd enjoying their thrills in the rest of the haunted house.

In the living room of the guesthouse, Sir Chadwick was going over his own plans with his allies. Hilda and Abby were seated, while Mandini, Starlight, and Jack Elvin leaned against the walls. The elves sat on the floor.

"Captain Starlight knows more about storms of the sea than any of us," he began. "So, I think we'll listen to his advice first."

Captain Starlight stood up. "I feel a bit odd lecturing Light Witches on witchcraft, but if that's what you want, so be it."

He plunged his hands deep into the pockets of his trousers and for a moment rocked on the heels of his sea boots.

"From what I've learned, there are only two ways to make a storm by witchcraft," he began. "You either anger the sea and she retaliates, or you ask the sea to grant you a favor.

"Ancient people — Greeks, Romans, and suchlike — believed it was the work of the Sea God. They didn't know it was the sea itself that decides."

"So, is the sea good or bad, Captain?" asked Mandini.

Starlight smiled. "Men have always asked that question, my friend. I don't know for sure, but I have an opinion."

"And what's your opinion, Adam?" asked Sir Chadwick.

Starlight thought for a bit. "The sea has always been good to me, but I've known it to be harsh to others. The Sea Witches love it and would choose no other life. I believe the sea is good to those who love it. And harsh to those who fear it."

"I knew a dog like that once," said Spike, and everybody laughed.

"So, will Wolfbane ask the sea to help him or will he anger it?" said Hilda when the laughter died down.

"He's already decided to anger it," replied Starlight.

"How do you know?" they all chorused.

"Benbow told me," Starlight said. "This morning he saw Wolfbane and his mother dumping Black Dust far out in the bay. It was already killing the fish around them. I think Wolfbane has devised some outrage against the sea, and the sea will strike back, sure enough."

"And kill innocent people in the process," said Sir Chadwick softly. "That sounds like Night Witch work, right enough." He stood up. "Thank you, Adam. Now, this is what I intend us to do. Spike, during this evening's performance, I want you to be on the Atlantis Boat, close to the pier. She's sturdy enough to weather any storm. You must keep her close to the theater and then, when the show is coming to an end, sprinkle Ice Dust on the sea."

"I understand," Spike answered.

Sir Chadwick continued. "Adam, I want you backstage, with us."

Captain Starlight nodded.

"Mandini, I have arranged for you to repeat your performance tonight, so you will be there on hand as well." He smiled. "Naturally, the management is delighted."

Mandini gave a brief bow.

"What about Abby and me, Chadwick?" Hilda asked.

"Abby, you, Hilda, Mandini, and myself will form a Light Witch circle in the wings as soon as the storm begins. If we succeed in stopping it, Wolfbane may try something else. We shall have to be ready for anything. Remember, we also have the elves on our side, and we all know how much Night Witches dread being tickled by them."

"An ace up our sleeves," said Mandini, and a white dove fluttered from his hands to emphasize his remark.

32

Captain Starlight
Saves the Day

When it was time to go to the theater, Abby and Spike walked along the promenade with their friends. Jack Elvin walked with the elves and Sir Chadwick and Hilda linked arms, while Captain Starlight, Spike, and Mandini chatted to one another.

It did not seem possible to Abby that a storm was coming. The sea was calm and the evening sun shone like beaten gold on the dappled waters, but they could see people on the edge of the incoming tide, looking at the dead fish that were being washed ashore.

Abby walked beside Jack Elvin and Lupin. She put her hands into the pockets of her sailor suit and found some of the golden berries she had picked in Darkwood Forest that afternoon.

"Look at these, Lupin," she said. "I saw a unicorn eating some today."

Lupin looked down at her hand and stopped quite still. "Where did you get those?" he asked in a hushed voice.

"Darkwood Forest," she answered.

All the elves gathered around her in an excited circle. The

others stopped to see what the fuss was about, and Lupin held up one of the berries he had taken from Abby's hand. "Look, Jack," he cried out. "Elfberries! Abby has found elfberries in Darkwood Forest!"

"Why are they so special?" asked Abby, puzzled by the elves' excitement.

"That's what we've been looking for since we left the Hardcastle estate," said Lupin. "Wood elves can only live where elfberries grow. You've found us a new home, Abby."

"Well, it was Paddy the Pooka, really," Abby said. But no one was listening.

"A good omen for the rest of the night," said Sir Chadwick, and they hurried on.

The show went particularly well that evening. By now, Abby's song had become a firm favorite with the tourists, and they joined in and sang along during Abby's encore. Mandini surpassed himself and had the audience gasping at his feats of magic.

When the melodrama was over, Sir Chadwick said to Abby, "We'll just have time to change during Mr. Ching's sword-swallowing act. Hurry back to the wings, and we'll form the Light Witch circle while Jack and the elves are doing their act."

"I'll wait with Mandini," whispered Hilda, who was also backstage.

"The sea appears to be getting rougher," said Mandini. "I've just taken a look outside."

"And there's a curious light to the south," said Starlight, who had joined them.

"Where's Benbow?" Abby said, suddenly anxious.

Starlight pointed into the rafters and Abby saw Benbow perched high above.

Mr. Ching, the Amazing Oriental Gentleman, began his act with some astonishing feats of fire-eating. Gasps came from the auditorium as he blew great arcs of fire-across the stage. Then, for his finale, he swallowed a gleaming sword.

After his last bow, Mr. Ching stood in the wings as Jack Elvin and the dancing elves clattered onto the stage in their tap shoes.

"I like to watch these little guys perform, Abby," said Mr. Ching in a broad London accent.

"So do I, Mr. Ching," Abby replied as she joined Sir Chadwick, Mandini, and Hilda in the Light Witch circle.

"Hold hands," instructed Sir Chadwick. "Concentrate on holding back the storm."

As Jack and the elves danced, Abby could hear a distant howling of the wind growing louder and louder above the clatter of tiny feet on the stage.

"Concentrate harder," said Sir Chadwick as the theater began to shake. The audience looked around uneasily, but the band continued to play and Jack and the elves danced on.

When they reached the end of their performance, the theater was shaking as though a great hand held the pier in its grasp. The people in the audience were looking decidedly unhappy.

The band was just about to begin the national anthem when, suddenly, Sir Morden leaped up onto the stage. He tore off the jovial butcher's face mask and confronted Jack Elvin.

"Prepare to die, you common little swine!" he shouted, and drew the sword from his walking stick.

The audience gasped in surprise but assumed it was all part of the show. Several began to whistle and clap with approval.

Sir Morden advanced on Jack Elvin, thrusting with his sword. Jack backed away, trying to keep the elves safely behind him.

Seeing that Jack was about to be killed, Sir Chadwick broke away from the Light Witch circle and seized Mr. Ching's sword.

Sir Morden was about to make a fatal thrust when his blade was parried by Sir Chadwick's weapon.

Sir Morden's eyes blazed with rage. "Get out of my way, you fool. This is real life, not acting," he snarled.

"I wondered where you were, Wolfbane," replied Sir Chadwick, mistaking Sir Morden for his brother.

"Don't call me Wolfbane. As you are about to die, you might wish to know that the name of your executioner is Sir Morden Hardcastle."

Sir Chadwick raised an eyebrow.

"Well, we'll see if you can fence any better than your brother," he answered. The two swords clashed, and the men began to fight back and forth across the stage. The audience found this extra spectacle tremendously exciting and cheered wildly, despite the alarming rocking of the theater.

Since Sir Chadwick had broken away from the Light Witch circle, the storm was raging with even greater ferocity. It felt even more as though they were being shaken by some giant hand.

Morden tried every trick he knew, but it soon became clear that Sir Chadwick was the better swordsman. With a final twirling motion of his own sword, Sir Chadwick caused Morden's blade to fly from his hand and stick quivering into the boards of the stage.

Suffused with rage, Morden was not about to give up. He seized Lupin with one hand and swept him off his feet. Holding the elf above his head, he backed over to the window. "Come here, Jack Elvin," he shouted, "or I'll toss this little creature into the sea."

But Morden had underestimated the elves. They all rushed forward and began to tickle him. Morden gave a ghastly laugh and was forced to drop Lupin.

Glancing around in a savage rage, he remembered the vial Lucia had given him. He quickly swallowed the contents and advanced toward Jack Elvin.

Sir Chadwick reached for his wand, and everyone in the theater screamed in horror as they saw Sir Morden Hardcastle undergo a startling transformation. His face, contorted with rage, became that of a snarling wolf. Teeth bared to kill and bloodshot eyes fixed on Jack Elvin, he raised his front paws, which were armed with long vicious claws.

He was almost upon Jack when there was a sudden crash of shattering glass as one of the windows burst open.

The massive arm of a giant octopus slithered in through the opening. Thick as a tree trunk, it snaked wildly about the auditorium. The long waving tentacle groped blindly for something to ensnare.

It found Sir Morden and lifted him, struggling and terrified, into the air.

Morden the wolf tried to bite the wavering tentacle, but to no avail. He gave one long terrible scream as he was dragged through the broken window and out into the blackness of the storm-ravaged night.

Above the roar of the wind came the fearful shouts and screams of the audience as more windows around the auditorium smashed in and two other tentacles thrust into the theater. The whole structure was groaning now as the giant octopus strained to uproot the entire pier.

"How can we fight it?" shouted Mandini above the pandemonium.

Captain Starlight bellowed, "Benbow, bring my harpoon from the Atlantis Boat!"

Benbow swooped down from the rafters and flew out through one of the shattered windows. The great bird hovered for a moment above the raging sea until he found Spike, riding the storm-tossed waves in the Atlantis Boat below the pier.

Benbow swooped down into the cabin. Seconds later he emerged, carrying Starlight's harpoon in his beak. The giant octopus, half out of the water and clinging to the pier, tried to strike him with a tentacle but Benbow was too fast. He flew back into the theater and dropped the weapon into Captain Starlight's waiting hands.

The Time Witches

"Give me all the Ice Dust you've got," Starlight commanded.

The Light Witches each took a handful from their pockets.

"Sprinkle it on the blade," Starlight instructed calmly.

The harpoon glowed with a blue light, but the theater continued to rock violently.

"I must get up onto the roof," the captain said. "I can't see him clearly from in here."

"I know the way. Follow me," shouted Abby above the roaring of the storm. She led Captain Starlight to a flight of stairs that ended in a trapdoor in the ceiling.

She scrambled up to open it, and they went quickly up into the attic of the onion dome.

"Take this ladder," Abby shouted, and they climbed up to a door that led out onto a balcony around the dome of the theater. A fearsome sight confronted them.

With the storm raging all around, the giant octopus, half out of the water, clung with its tentacle to the roof of the pier as it tried to wrench the structure into the raging sea.

Abby could see one of the octopus's great eyes, staring balefully from its monstrous head, just a few yards away. The creature was still trying to rip the whole structure down. Spike, in the Atlantis Boat, was battling to keep the craft away from one of the flailing arms.

Suddenly, a tentacle whipped up and encircled Abby's waist. Her feet left the ground. But before she could shout out, Captain Starlight hurled his harpoon into the creature's gaping mouth.

The air filled with an unearthly screeching wail, louder even than the raging storm. Abby felt the tentacle loosen its grip, and she fell back to the platform with a thud.

The terrible screaming continued as the creature slowly released its hold on the pier and shrank back into the sea.

Abby and Starlight went below and found the theater in chaos. The storm had died down, but the audience was still in a state of panic. Several people had fainted.

Abby and Captain Starlight joined Sir Chadwick in the wings.

"I think I'd better calm them down," said Mandini, strolling onto the stage. He leaned forward toward the orchestra pit and said to the conductor, "Maestro, a drumroll, if you please."

At the sound, the hysteria started to die down and Mandini stepped forward.

"Ladies and gentlemen, may I have your attention," he said in a booming voice.

The audience gazed at him expectantly.

"Thank you," said Mandini. He began to wave his hands. "Now, if you will all look into my eyes . . . you are all falling asleep . . . a deep soothing sleep."

Abby watched as the people in the audience slowly closed their eyes.

"When you wake up," Mandini continued, "you will re-member only that there was a great storm that broke the win-dows of the theater. You saw nothing else. Nothing! When I snap my fingers, you will come to your senses again and re-member only what I have told you."

Mandini snapped his fingers. The people rose from their seats and began to leave in an orderly fashion, chatting to one another about the dreadful weather.

When they had all left, Sir Chadwick spoke to his compan-ions. "Any sign of Wolfbane?" he asked.

They all shook their heads.

"Well, at least we've thwarted his plan for tonight," he said, looking about him at the battered auditorium. "But tomorrow is another day."

On the dark roof of the spiral slide, far above the crowds enjoying the fair below, Wolfbane stood with his mother in the darkness. "I'm sorry about your other son, Mother," he said nonchalantly. "But he did want to do everything his own way. He wasted your spell, just turning himself into a wolf."

Lucia Cheeseman shrugged. "I suppose that's what comes of being brought up as an aristocrat," she said. "They sometimes underestimate the opposition. Sir Chadwick Street and his friends are a slippery bunch."

"They'll not outwit you and me, Mother. Just one more day and we'll remake history."

As his mother cackled appreciatively, Wolfbane looked toward the horizon where the last of the storm flickered like the flames of a dying fire.

33

An Outing by Train

The morning after the storm, Sir Chadwick, Hilda, and Abby strolled along the promenade in sparkling sunshine. Workmen were replacing the flowers in the baskets hanging from the gas lamps and repairing the floral clock.

On the pier, they could see Mr. Greenbower supervising the installation of new windows in the theater. Obviously, he had found another new source of income.

"Well, we've changed everything around here. There's no doubt about that," Sir Chadwick said, and he twirled the wand he carried like a cane.

"No rocks and pebbles on the beach," said Hilda. "And the pier is still standing."

As they were passing the fair, Abby noticed that the carousel was still closed, although a man seemed to be working on it.

Sir Chadwick fished in his pockets for their return tickets and gave them a glance. "Not much time left," he said.

"There's still the elves to settle in their new home," Abby reminded him.

Sir Chadwick nodded as they walked along the pier to where the Atlantis Boat was moored.

"Yes," he answered. "I've been giving that some thought as well."

When they reached the ladder at the end of the pier, they could see that Captain Starlight, Mandini, and Spike were fishing from the deck of the Atlantis Boat.

"The water's clear and calm again," Starlight said when they joined them on deck. "Benbow reported that there's no sign of the octopus, either."

"I pity the poor creature," Sir Chadwick said. "It was all Wolfbane's fault. I blame him for the abomination he made of it."

"What about the elves?" asked Mandini, laying aside his rod.

"Yes," said Sir Chadwick. "I've decided what we'll do. Do any of you know anything about train engines?"

"I know a little bit about them," said Captain Starlight, as he cast his line farther into the sea. "I worked for a time on the Baltimore and Ohio railroad and on a Mississippi steamboat."

"Did you, Adam?" said Sir Chadwick, impressed. "I always think of you as a seafaring man. The problem is," continued Sir Chadwick, "we have to get the families of the elves from Merlin College, Oxford, to Darkwood Forest. It occurs to me that the best method would be by train."

"Won't it cause a bit of a stir?" said Mandini. "All those little guys getting off the regular service to Oxford. And when they turn up with all their families for the return journey . . ." He shrugged. "It would puzzle people, surely?"

"Not if we used a ghost train," said Sir Chadwick with a smile.

He stood up. "Come on, we have to make our excuses about missing tonight's performance. Then we're going on a short trip."

Sir Chadwick refused to answer any further questions. Instead, once they'd collected Jack Elvin and the elves, he led the entire party to the train station.

"Abby, Spike, Hilda, Captain Starlight, Mandini, Jack Elvin, and seven elves," he muttered, counting on his fingers. Then he gestured to the ticket clerk. "Thirteen return tickets to Speller, please," he ordered.

"You forgot yourself, dearest," said Hilda.

Sir Chadwick slapped his forehead. "Sorry, fourteen tickets."

"How many children?" asked the clerk.

"Two."

The clerk looked puzzled. "Are all those little ones adults?" he asked.

"I'll have you know we're all husbands and fathers, my good man," said Lupin indignantly.

"No offense intended," said the clerk hastily. "Did you want cheap day-returns?"

Sir Chadwick sighed. "I had no idea this would be so complicated," he muttered. "Yes, yes, cheap day-returns, if you please."

"You'd better get a move on," said the clerk. "The train's about to depart."

The journey didn't take very long. On the platform of Speller station, Sir Chadwick said, "Follow me."

He led them behind the station to a yard where there was a large patch of ground overgrown with weeds.

A rusty spur from the main line crossed the ground. Sticking up through the overgrowth, on either side of the rails, were great rusting lumps: a variety of wheels and cogs, a dented boiler, and piles of long, unidentifiable lengths of metal.

"What's all this?" asked Jack Elvin.

Sir Chadwick gestured around him. "It was the *Torgate Belle*, until it derailed coming out of the tunnel twenty years ago. The driver was trying to break the record time to London. After the crash, the railway company dumped all the remains here."

"And we're going to get it to run again?" asked Captain Starlight.

"Right first time," said Sir Chadwick. Then he consulted Jack Elvin. "You're the engineer, Jack. Just tell us what to do."

Jack studied the remains of the train for a while, then he made some quick sketches in a notebook. "First make a pile of all the wheels," he said.

"Light Witches, form a circle and hold hands," instructed Sir Chadwick, and under Jack's direction, Mandini, Hilda, Abby, and Sir Chadwick began to will the pieces of machinery into assorted piles.

Lupin and the other elves sat watching the work, highly entertained as the piles of metal seemed to sort themselves into some logical order.

Activated by the power of Light Witch Will, the lumps of metal floated through the air as though they were no heavier than feathers. Quite soon, a recognizable train took shape. But it was thick with rust and dented all over.

"Can you restore everything to its original condition now?" asked Jack.

"Oh, I think so," replied Sir Chadwick, and rusty metal was soon transformed to gleaming newness.

"Now I need a big oil can," said Jack, and one was instantly produced. He set to work on various parts of the engine until he finally announced, "Water and coal and we're ready to go."

Abby looked at him with admiration and pride — her great-great-grandfather — even if she couldn't tell him!

Mandini gestured toward a cloud on the horizon, and it scudded toward them. He waved his hands again and directed a torrential stream of water into the engine's boiler.

Then he pointed to a corner of the yard. The earth erupted as lumps of coal burst from the ground and piled into the tender behind the engine.

They all stood back and admired their work, and Lupin led the elves in giving three cheers. The engine, complete with one carriage, stood on the spur line, resplendent in all its former glory.

"As good as new," said Sir Chadwick, looking on with approval. "I'll just borrow some matches from the stationmaster to light the boiler."

"Why doesn't he use magic to light it?" Jack Elvin asked Abby.

The Time Witches

"Light Witches only use magic when they have to," she explained. "We try to be like human beings as much as possible."

"When should we start for Oxford?" asked Spike.

"After nightfall," said Sir Chadwick. "Meanwhile, we'll need a railway timetable to warn us of other traffic on the line." He nodded to Spike and Abby. "While we plan the journey, why don't you two take the elves into Darkwood Forest and show them where you found the elfberry tree?"

"How far is it?" Spike asked Abby.

"A bit of a walk. I wish we had Paddy here," she replied.

"Over here, me darlin'," said a voice behind her.

Paddy, in his disguise as the old donkey, was hitched to a cart in the corner of the yard.

"Paddy," said Abby happily. "Do you think you could take Spike, me, and the elves to where we saw the unicorns?"

"Quick as a tinker's cuss," he answered. "Pile in me cart, now."

Abby, Spike, and the elves climbed aboard, and Paddy set off at a brisk trot toward Darkwood Forest.

Captain Starlight watched them depart with a sense of concern. "Benbow, keep an eye on them," he called out.

The great bird rose into the air and followed.

34

A Visit to Merlin College

O nce Paddy had turned from the Torgate Road into the forest and trotted deeper along the path through the woods, the elves began to chatter excitedly.

"This is a very nice forest," said Lupin. "Part of the old wild wood, you know."

"The wild wood?" asked Spike and Abby together.

Lupin nodded. "Once the wild wood covered almost the whole country."

"Before the humans came and made farms and towns," said Bramble.

"There were bears and wolves here in those days, too," Apple chimed in.

"And the elves were everywhere," added Gooseberry.

"We know some elves who live in London," said Abby.

"Do you mean Wooty and his chums?" said Acorn.

"Yes," replied Abby. "Do you know him?"

"He's my cousin, actually," said Lupin. "But town elves are a bit different from us. They *like* to eat dried elfberries. We prefer ours fresh from the tree."

"They like muffins and chocolate cake, too," said Spike.

They passed the stream where Abby had had the picnic

with Hilda and Sir Chadwick. After a time, Paddy entered the clearing where the elfberry tree grew.

Now the elves were almost beside themselves with delight as they leaped down from the cart. They surrounded the tree and carefully picked some of the berries and put them in their pockets.

"I haven't seen any unicorns yet," said Spike.

"They're behind you," Paddy whispered.

Spike and Abby glanced around to see the pure white horses watching them.

"Gosh," said Spike softly. "They *are* beautiful."

"I wish we could talk to them," said Abby.

"I'll translate, if you like," said Lupin. He called out in his own language and the unicorns came closer. They began to gently neigh and snort. Lupin suddenly looked worried.

He turned to Spike and Abby and said, "There are Night Witches in the forest."

"What are they doing?" asked Abby, alarmed.

"Something underground," answered Lupin after more conversation with the unicorns. "They aren't sure exactly, because the Night Witches have dug a big burrow. They've also planted a poison path all around it."

"What's a poison path?" asked Spike.

"Night Witches do it to keep us away," said Lupin. "They fear elves in case we come and tickle them in their sleep. So when they suspect we're about, they cover the ground they use with poison, but it also kills all the trees."

"I think Benbow and I had better go and take a look," said Abby. "Sir Chadwick will want to know about anything Wolfbane is up to."

"I'll stay here with Paddy and the elves," said Spike.

"Be careful," said Abby.

"I'll keep an eye on them, darlin'," said Paddy.

Lupin spoke once more to the unicorns before they trotted away.

"They told me where the burrow is. I'll come, too, and show you the way," said Lupin. "If Benbow can manage me as well."

"Easily, but you'll have to hang on tight," said Abby, and she called Benbow down.

They soared into the air and, as Abby whistled her tune, the three of them vanished.

"Over to the left, down there," Lupin said as Benbow flew them over the forest just above the level of the treetops.

Abby could now see a great ugly rise in the ground covered in dead trees, some of which had toppled to the ground. It looked as if a terrible battle had been fought in the forest. There was no sign of Wolfbane or any other Night Witch.

"Take us back to the elfberry tree, Benbow," Abby instructed.

When they returned to the clearing, Abby, Spike, and the elves climbed back into Paddy's cart, and they set off quickly back to Speller station.

Sir Chadwick, Jack Elvin, Mandini, and Captain Starlight were in the stationmaster's tiny office, poring over a railway map and a thick book containing train timetables.

Abby told Sir Chadwick about the strange burrow in Darkwood Forest.

"I think we'd better worry about that tomorrow," he said after giving it some thought. "Our first priority is to get the elves into their new home." He turned to Jack Elvin. "Is the train ready to depart?"

"She certainly is," said Jack.

Sir Chadwick remembered something else. "I think we'd better warn the Master of Merlin College that we're coming to collect his guests."

"Should we send Benbow with a note?" suggested Abby.

"Good idea," replied Sir Chadwick, but then he spotted something on the desk. "No, wait a moment." He pointed to the contraption and asked the stationmaster, "Is that a telegraph machine?"

"It is, sir."

"Does anyone know Morse code? Mine is a bit rusty."

"I do," said Captain Starlight.

"Excellent, Adam," said Sir Chadwick. "Please send the following message to the Master of Merlin College. His cable address is Mercol, if my memory still serves me:

"MERCOL STOP ARRIVING BY TRAIN TONIGHT TO EVACUATE ELVES STOP BEST WISHES STOP STREETWITCH STOP"

Captain Starlight tapped rapidly on the Morse key and the message was sent. There was a moment's pause, then an incoming signal started on the machine. Starlight wrote down the message and then read it aloud.

"ATTENTION STREETWITCH STOP DO NOT GO TO OXFORD STATION STOP HAVE ARRANGED FOR A SPECIAL BRANCH LINE TO ENTER COLLEGE GROUNDS STOP TAKE SPUR LINE MARKED MERLIN COLLEGE STOP REGARDS MERCOL STOP"

"How considerate of the Master of Merlin College to put in a branch line just for us," said Sir Chadwick. "Now if everybody is ready, all aboard the *Torgate Belle*."

Jack Elvin, Mandini, and Captain Starlight were all in the locomotive. Mandini claimed he'd always wanted to be a fireman and stoke a train engine's boiler. He had acquired a large gleaming shovel and was anxious to get to work. The *Torgate Belle* pulled out onto the main line and as darkness fell on the countryside, they headed toward Oxford.

It was warm in the plush interior of the Pullman carriage and, after a while, Abby, Spike, and the elves drifted into sleep. Abby had a strange dream in which she was being chased by something fearful she could not see. But she knew it came from the ugly burrow that Wolfbane had made in Darkwood Forest.

There was no one else in the dream but she kept hearing a voice repeating, "Go into the tunnel, Abby," over and over again. Then she felt a hand gently shaking her shoulder.

It was Sir Chadwick. "Wake up, Abby," he said softly. "We're on the spur line for Merlin College."

Abby and Spike looked out of the carriage window and saw that a full moon shone down on the countryside. They could see farms and villages in the silvery light. Abby noticed that the tracks the *Torgate Belle* ran upon were not actually resting on the ground. The rails soared over the meadows on the outskirts of Oxford.

"Look, Spike," Abby said excitedly pointing below. "The River Thames."

Sir Chadwick stood beside them. "They call the Thames the Isis when it flows through Oxford, children," he explained.

"Why?" asked Spike.

Sir Chadwick smiled. "They always like to do things a little differently at Oxford," he said.

"Aren't the buildings old?" said Abby, looking down on the ancient stone of the sleeping colleges.

"Yes, and Merlin College is the oldest," replied Sir Chadwick proudly.

The train started to slow down and gradually came to a stop as they passed over a high brick wall surrounding a group of ancient buildings set in a very large garden.

Abby and Spike could see tree-lined lawns and a large lake dappled with moonlight. In the center of the lawn waited a group of men and women, dressed in beautiful robes of scarlet and silver with flat-topped hats. They were surrounded by groups of little people.

The families of the seven elves were all waving enthusiastically to Lupin and his companions.

Sir Chadwick descended from the train and raised his hat to the most imposing figure. "Delighted to see you again, Master," he said.

"Welcome back to Merlin College, Chadwick," he replied, warmly. "And Hilda Bluebell and Mandini are with you. How nice to see our old graduates."

Sir Chadwick now introduced Doctor Horace Gomble to Captain Starlight, Jack Elvin, Spike, and Abby. He was an imposing man with a broad chest and vast ginger side-whiskers.

"Delighted to be back, Master," replied Sir Chadwick, with a note of respect in his voice that Abby had rarely heard before.

Many handshakes were exchanged before Doctor Gomble

suggested they should retire to the dons' common room. "It's a pity you couldn't come earlier," he said. "You could have dined with us."

"I'm afraid urgent matters press upon us, Master," said Sir Chadwick.

"We'll stay with our families in the garden, if you don't mind," said Lupin.

"I thought dons were always men," Spike whispered to Abby as they walked behind two rather stately ladies dressed splendidly in scarlet robes.

Although Spike had spoken softly, Doctor Gomble had heard his remark.

"Merlin College has admitted lady Light Witches since the fourteenth century," he said. "And we are rather pleased to have them."

The two lady dons smiled.

The party walked through ancient corridors until they entered the dons' common room. A log fire burned despite its being summer. The walls were oak-paneled and hung with portraits. Silver glittered on the sideboards and the room was filled with old leather chairs.

One of the dons said a few sentences of welcome in a strange, whistling and grunting language that sounded vaguely familiar to Abby.

"What language do you think he was speaking?" she asked Spike.

"The language of the Seven Seas," he whispered. "I think it was for my benefit, but he has a very unusual accent."

Doctor Gomble raised his head. "Please forgive my companion's lack of skill, Your Highness," he said to Spike. "We poor scholars have little chance to practice the proper accent of the language, living, as we do, so far inland."

"On the contrary," said Spike, suddenly becoming quite gracious. "The accent was quite correct. It is the one used by the aristocrats of Lantua. Whales and dolphins use a more relaxed pronunciation."

A waiter served drinks from sparkling crystal decanters. After some polite gossip about the college, Doctor Gomble looked to Sir Chadwick. "So, tell me, how goes the battle with Wolfbane?" he asked.

Sir Chadwick shrugged. "We do our best, Master. We've had some measure of success."

Doctor Gomble looked at him with a sudden shrewd expression. "And you are about to have a major confrontation, I believe?"

"That is correct," Sir Chadwick confirmed, then bowed to Doctor Gomble. "That is why I have a special request to make. May we consult the sword?"

Doctor Gomble nodded and put down his empty glass. "I was expecting just such a request. Arrangements have been made. I have already sent for the keeper of the other key."

He stood up and the undergraduates all rose to bow as the diners at the head table departed from the hall.

"A *sword?*" said Spike, mystified. "We're going to consult a *sword?*"

But this time Doctor Gomble chose not to hear.

35

The Voice from the Sword

Sir Chadwick, Jack Elvin, Abby, Spike, Mandini, Captain Starlight, and the dons all followed Doctor Gomble across the moonlit quadrangle to a small arched doorway set in a wall covered with ivy.

"You are about to enter the most hallowed ground in Merlin College," Doctor Gomble said to them all in a hushed voice.

He took a large key from his pocket and tried to turn it in the keyhole. "No one has been in here for nearly a hundred years," he said apologetically. "The lock is a bit stiff." And he continued to struggle.

"I would have thought *this* was a case for using magic," said Jack Elvin to Mandini, where they stood at the back of the crowd.

Mandini shook his head. "Of all the Light Witches, dons of Merlin College use magic least," he explained. "In fact, they relish using human methods, like communicating by telegram."

"That's why it was such a great honor that they made the special railway tracks for us," said Hilda.

"Did you study at Merlin as well, Hilda?" asked Abby. "I

thought you had worked in the store and then become an actress."

"I had a leave of absence from the theater. All Light Witches must go to Merlin College, Abby," she said. "You will, too, one day."

"I wonder where I will stay?" said Abby.

"Over there, on the second staircase," said Doctor Gomble, pointing across the quadrangle while still struggling with the key.

Finally, it turned, and the door creaked open to reveal a steep flight of stairs descending into darkness.

"Oh, dear. I quite forgot about the lack of lights. It's been some time since I visited," said the doctor.

"Allow me," said Captain Starlight as he produced a glowing glass bottle of Saint Elmo's fire from his pocket. Leading the way, Starlight led them down and down the long staircase until they entered a high, vaulted brick chamber that was some sort of junction.

Tunnels led off in all directions. From one came a wheezing sound. It grew louder and louder, until a familiar figure mounted on a bicycle entered the main chamber.

It was Polartius, the librarian in charge of all Light Witch records. Long white hair flowed over his shoulders and was tucked into the pockets of his frock coat.

"I'm afraid I'm late," the old gentleman said, dismounting with some difficulty and brushing off his dusty coat. Peering over the spectacles perched on his long, thin nose, he took in the assembled crowd and said, "Sorry, Master. I took a bit of a tumble under Beaconsfield. Parts of the London tunnel are in a sorry state of disrepair."

"Did you remember the key?" asked Doctor Gomble.

"Of course," Polartius replied, holding up a silver object on the end of a length of chain.

Doctor Gomble explained to the others. "We keep the two keys to the room at different places for security reasons."

Polartius propped his bicycle against a wall and continued to dust himself off.

"Hello, Polartius," said Abby. Gesturing toward Spike, she asked, "Do you remember us?"

"Of course not," he replied. "I don't meet you until the century after this one."

"Oh, yes," said Abby. "Sometimes I forget."

"Don't worry," he said in a more kindly voice. "You will get over it in the future."

"This way," said Doctor Gomble, leading them down another tunnel. After a time they came to an ancient door, iron-bound and set with two keyholes. Doctor Gomble used one key and Polartius the other.

The door swung open, but instead of being in a room as Abby had expected, they were standing in a woodland glade. The sun was shining and birds were singing. In the middle of the clearing, lit by a shaft of sunshine, stood a large granite boulder. Embedded in its very center was a great sword that shone with a silvery light.

"*Excalibur,*" said Abby softly.

"You recognize the sword of King Arthur?" said Doctor Gomble.

"Oh, yes," said Abby. "My mother told me the story."

"This is the most precious possession that Merlin College guards," said Doctor Gomble. "It was placed here by Merlin himself, who gave us the keys."

"I thought King Arthur returned it to the lake," said Spike, who was also familiar with the legend.

"Yes," said Gomble, "it was the lake in the college garden." He now faced the others. "Each of you may hold the handle of the sword for a moment," he explained. "But it will have a message for only one of you."

The dons stood back as Abby's companions stepped forward one by one and grasped the hilt. Each shook their head as they walked away.

Abby was the last. When she took hold of the jeweled hilt, she felt a sharp tingle in her arm, and the deep voice of a man spoke inside her head.

The voice said, "Go into the tunnel, Abby — even though others wish you to go another way."

She let go of the handle. "I heard a voice, it said —"

"Don't tell us, child," Doctor Gomble interrupted quickly. "The message was for you alone."

"But I don't understand what it means."

"You will, Abby," said Sir Chadwick. "And now we must go back to Darkwood Forest."

They returned to the train and said their good-byes. Chattering excitedly, the elf families climbed aboard and, with a final wave to the assembled Master and dons, Mandini released the brakes and they set off on the return journey.

Abby looked down at Oxford as they passed over the countryside again, the rail tracks vanishing behind the *Torgate Belle*. In a few minutes, they had rejoined the main line and were heading back toward Darkwood Forest.

36

A New Home
for the Elves

The Great Mandini and Captain Starlight said they
would like to handle the controls of the *Torgate Belle*,
so Jack Elvin rode in the Pullman carriage. Hilda sat
with the elf children. Fascinated to discover that their language contained quite a lot of birdcalls, she was teaching them
a birdsong.

Spike and Abby chatted with Lupin, Bramble, and Acorn
while Sir Chadwick sat looking out of the window at the
moonlit countryside, deep in thought. Eventually, Jack Elvin
joined him.

"You looked worried," he said.

Sir Chadwick smiled quickly. "A problem I'm wrestling
with," he explained.

"Would you like to talk about it?" Jack offered.

Sir Chadwick nodded. "It's our return journey through
time. I'm deeply concerned about how vulnerable we'll be."

"Why?" asked Jack.

Sir Chadwick sat up straighter. "Hilda, Abby, and I will
make the journey strictly according to the Wizards' rules.
That means no magic. It's totally forbidden. Even Ice Dust
won't work as we pass through time itself."

Jack understood the problem. "But Wolfbane isn't traveling the Wizards' way."

"Exactly," said Sir Chadwick. "By using Ma Hemlock's carriage, he's outside the Wizards' jurisdiction. He can use any villainy. We'll be totally at his mercy. My wand will be useless. We'll have no weapons to fight back."

"If we had the right chemicals, I could make you one," said Jack.

"How?" said Sir Chadwick, looking around. He could see nothing from which a weapon might be fashioned.

Standing up, Jack unhooked one of the small paraffin lamps from the carriage wall and removed the shade. "By filling this with an explosive mixture."

"But we don't have any chemicals to make explosives," said Sir Chadwick.

Abby and Spike had heard the conversation. "I think I know how we could get some, Sir Chadwick," said Abby.

Jack and Sir Chadwick looked up and Abby continued, "Lupin, Bramble, and Acorn just told us they used to be Fetcher elves before they lived in Morden Hardcastle's forest," said Abby.

"Fetchers!" exclaimed Sir Chadwick. "Were they, by Jove?"

"I don't understand," said Jack, puzzled.

Sir Chadwick explained. "Elves have always been friends and helpers to Light Witches. Old-fashioned Light Witches who live in remote places are helped by certain elves called Fetchers. They fetch the ingredients used in spells."

"So they could bring us what we need," said Jack.

"They'd need about fifteen minutes when we get to the next town," said Sir Chadwick.

"That quick?"

"Certainly," said Lupin who, together with Hilda and the other elves, had joined them.

Hilda went forward to tell Starlight to stop the train, while Jack held up the lamp. "Bring me enough saltpeter to fill this to here," Jack said, indicating with his hand the amount he required.

"Saltpeter?" repeated Lupin, Bramble, and Acorn, mystified.

Sir Chadwick slapped his forehead. "Oh, dear. They would only know the ancient Light Witch names. And I've quite forgotten them."

"I can remember," said Abby. "I've just done Ancient Terms in Light Witch lessons. The word for saltpeter is *cobat*."

Jack shifted his hand higher. "And enough sulfur to fill it to here."

"*Baltrimat,*" translated Abby.

"Then sufficient charcoal to fill it to the brim."

"We understand the word *charcoal*," said Acorn.

The train slowed to a halt and the elves jumped off.

"How will they find all that in fifteen minutes?" asked Spike.

Sir Chadwick smiled. "Fetcher elves can find anything," he replied. "That's what happens to most of the stuff that human beings think they lose."

"But where will they look?" asked Spike.

Sir Chadwick pointed out of the window. "There's a small town over there. The school will have chemicals for their science classes and there'll be a pharmacy on the main street."

Within ten minutes, the elves had returned with the ingredients Jack had requested. He carefully mixed them together and packed the result into the lamp. "May I have your pocket watch and the box of matches you took from the stationmaster at Speller?" he asked Sir Chadwick.

The train started again and Jack took a clasp knife from his pocket. It had all sorts of special blades. He selected a screwdriver and set to work. In quite a short time, he held up the lamp. "That should work," he said.

The winder of the watch protruded slightly from a hole that Jack had bored in the lamp's casing with his clasp knife.

"When you want it to go off, press down on the watch winder. That will give you three seconds before it explodes."

"Most ingenious," Sir Chadwick said, placing the lamp in his pocket. "Thank you, Jack."

"What do you want it for, Sir Chadwick?" asked Abby.

"It may come in handy," he replied. "After all, we don't know exactly what Wolfbane has up his sleeve."

Jack could see that Abby was admiring the clasp knife he still held in his hand. He passed it to her. "Here's a present," he said with a smile, "because you have green eyes just like my mother."

"Have I?" said Abby, placing the knife carefully in the pocket where she kept a small handful of Ice Dust. "I often wondered where they came from."

But Jack didn't hear the last part of her remark, for his attention had returned to Sir Chadwick. "What's the plan now?" he asked.

Sir Chadwick looked from the window to where the first streaks of dawn were lighting the sky. "First, we shall drop the elves off in Darkwood Forest, then Captain Starlight, Spike, and Mandini will go back to the Atlantis Boat and return to the future. But you, Abby, Hilda, and I must go to the grade crossing at Speller station. You have to meet someone there, Jack. And that is when I think Wolfbane will make his move."

"Who am I going to meet?" asked Jack.

"I'd better not tell you that," said Sir Chadwick. "Let's hope events just take their proper course."

At sunrise, the *Torgate Belle* was approaching Speller. They passed the station and the level crossing and entered the tunnel to eventually emerge alongside Darkwood Forest. Captain Starlight and Mandini brought the train to a wheezing halt.

"Welcome to your new home," Sir Chadwick said to the elves as they stepped down from the train.

Lupin was the last one to shake hands with Jack Elvin. "We'll never forget what you have done for us, Jack," he said. "The elves will be special friends to you and your family forever."

After watching the families run off into the welcoming woods, Sir Chadwick gathered Starlight, Spike, and Mandini around him. "Time for you to go as well, my gallant friends," he said.

The three protested but Sir Chadwick held up his hand. "We can't break the Wizards' rules anymore," he said firmly. "Abby, Hilda, and I have tickets to be here in the past. But you don't have permission from the Wizards. So, we must face this final test without you."

Captain Starlight nodded. "You're right, of course, Chadwick," he said. "But Benbow is not ruled by Wizard law. He is a free agent and will stay with Abby."

The great bird, perched on the roof of the railway carriage, squawked his agreement.

"So be it," said Sir Chadwick. "Now, if you will first take us

The Time Witches

to Speller station, you must then go back to Torgate and the Atlantis Boat."

A few minutes later, the train wheezed to a halt by the grade crossing, and Hilda, Abby, and Sir Chadwick got off.

"What will you do with the *Torgate Belle?*" Abby called out as the train slowly huffed away.

"We'll leave her on platform two," shouted Mandini. "I'm sure the town will be glad to have her back."

And with that, they gathered speed and entered the tunnel.

Hilda, Jack, Abby, and Sir Chadwick walked to the station platform. "I wonder what the time is," said Sir Chadwick, reaching for his pocket watch. Then he remembered what Jack had done with it. "Oh well, we'll just have to use the station clock," he said.

They found the stationmaster cooking breakfast on the iron stove in his office. "Fancy some Speller bangers and a nice fresh egg?" he asked cheerfully.

"Speller sausages," said Sir Chadwick cheerily. "I would be delighted."

Over the meal, Abby thought about the message the sword of Merlin had given her. *Go into the tunnel, Abby — even though others wish you to go another way.* What could it mean?

She wondered if the tunnels under Merlin College that Polartius had used might be significant. She asked Sir Chadwick.

"The Wizard Ways?" he said. "I don't think there are any close by here. The nearest one I can think of comes out at Canterbury. Why do you ask?"

"No special reason," Abby replied. She wanted to tell Sir Chadwick what the sword had said to her but knew she mustn't.

"Some people believe the Wizard Ways were made by

Druids," Hilda told her. "Chadwick is right, though, there are none around here. Certain parts of the country are thick with them."

"I see," said Abby, still puzzling over the message from the sword.

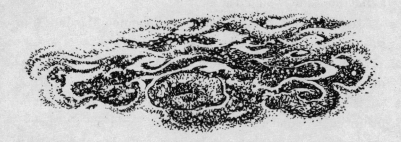

37

Jack Elvin Meets His Fate

The morning passed slowly in the station until at last the stationmaster announced, "The London train is due soon. Old Josiah Bowsprit is a bit late with his load of Ice Dust."

"Should we all go and take a look?" suggested Sir Chadwick, flexing his shoulders and loosening the wand tucked in his belt.

Abby, Hilda, Jack, and Sir Chadwick left the office and stood by the grade crossing. After a few minutes, they saw a figure escorting two pigs that were pulling a cart toward them.

One of the cart's wheels was wobbling and, just before it reached the railway line, it fell off. The cart toppled to one side, and boxes of Ice Dust fell into the dusty road.

Jack Elvin hurried forward to where Josiah Bowsprit was scratching his head. "Now, what am I going to do about this?" he said dolefully.

"It's not so bad," said Jack cheerfully. "We can soon fix it."

"You may be able to, young man," said Josiah sadly. "But it looks difficult enough to a common seafaring man such as myself."

"Let us take your packages into the station, sir, while Jack mends the wheel," offered Sir Chadwick.

Bowsprit smiled. "That's very decent of you," he said. "This must be my lucky day."

By the time Abby, Hilda, and Sir Chadwick had returned from delivering the packages, Jack had managed to replace the wheel and tighten the nut that kept it in place.

Mr. Bowsprit was delighted. "You're a very handy young man," he said thoughtfully. "I don't suppose you're looking for work?"

"Well, as a matter of fact, I am," said Jack.

Josiah Bowsprit paused, as if trying to make up his mind, then he pointed behind him. "You can't see it from here," he said. "But just behind that hill, there's a path that leads to the town of Speller. It's below the cliffs by the sea. And if I do say so myself, it's the finest place anyone would want to live. Now, we really need a clever, handy fellow such as yourself. What do you say?"

Jack smiled. "It sounds just right for me," he said. "But there's some business I've got to attend to here first."

"No, Jack," said Sir Chadwick firmly. "This meeting is meant to be. You must go with Josiah now."

"But I'm —" began Jack.

Before he could utter another word, Sir Chadwick sprinkled both Jack and Josiah Bowsprit with Ice Dust. "You will forget us and everything we did," he commanded. "Now, go to your destiny in Speller and don't look back."

The two men set off with the cart toward Speller.

Abby suddenly felt very sad. "Good-bye, Jack," she called out, adding softly, "I never did ask you about my great-great-great-grandmother with the green eyes."

Hilda put a comforting arm around her shoulder and Sir Chadwick said, "At least you'll have his penknife to remind you of him."

When Jack and Josiah were almost out of sight, there was a sudden crash of thunder, and lightning forked all around the station.

The spectral carriage appeared in the road. Wolfbane sat with his mother and looked down.

"You're too late, Wolfbane," said Sir Chadwick grimly, and stepped protectively in front of Hilda and Abby.

Wolfbane looked at the distant figures. "They're not quite in the sanctuary of Speller," he said haughtily. "Still time for me to demonstrate the superiority of Night Witch power."

"What is Night Witch power?" asked Sir Chadwick contemptuously. "You turned your back on kindness and decency and chose to exist in dirt, squalor, and cruelty. And all because the fear of those weaker than yourself makes you feel strong. You smell of many things, Wolfbane, but your strongest stench is the odor of cowardice."

More than anything, Wolfbane hated being insulted by Sir Chadwick. Every word was a blow to his pride.

"Yes," he hissed. "The power of cruelty is far preferable to the sanctimonious piety of a second-rate actor. You've seen too many plays, Chadwick Street. Only a deluded idiot would slave in the theater rather than rule over a kingdom of darkness."

Sir Chadwick threw his jacket to Hilda and drew his wand angrily.

"Get down and fight like a gentleman, Wolfbane!" he shouted.

Wolfbane glanced down with disdain. "Why should *I* fight with a clown when I have my creature to fight for me?"

He stood up and, spreading his cloak wide, shouted, "Baal, come forth."

There was an awful wrenching sound as a hillock bulged up in the level ground before them. Turf and earth erupted violently. One gigantic spider's leg sprang out of the ragged hole. More earth was torn away.

Abby gasped as Baal's head and hairy body emerged in their grotesque hugeness. The spider had grown to monstrous proportions.

"My lord!" exclaimed Sir Chadwick. "It's the size of an elephant."

"Thanks to my mother," Wolfbane gloated.

Sir Chadwick leaped forward and pulled him from the coach. Wolfbane tumbled to the ground but quickly recovered and reached for his own weapon. They began to fence back and forth. Sparks of Ice Dust and dark bursts of Black Dust erupted from their wands.

Lucia Cheeseman, still seated in the carriage, held Caspar in her lap. She threw the raven into the air, shouting, "Tear out his eyes!"

The creature flew toward Sir Chadwick's face with his talons extended.

But Hilda was too fast for Caspar. Swiftly, she reached out and caught the raven in Sir Chadwick's coat and threw it to the ground.

Lucia sprang to her feet, shrieking furiously, and launched herself at Hilda's back. But Hilda quickly stepped aside and Lucia thudded down on the road, knocking the wind out of herself.

When she attempted to get up, Hilda placed a foot firmly

on her back and forced her to lie facedown, squirming in the dusty road.

Wolfbane and Sir Chadwick continued to fight with savage intensity. Both had been taught to fence by the same master. Their skills appeared equal.

Abby and Hilda watched anxiously as the two battled ferociously. It was impossible to tell who would win.

While they fought, Baal stood quivering at the roadside, ready to aid its master.

At one moment, Abby thought Wolfbane would call on the creature to help him. But Wolfbane needed the spider for another task.

He backed away from Sir Chadwick's flashing wand and, pointing toward Jack and Josiah Bowsprit, who were still on the path to Speller, screamed, "Kill them, Baal!"

The spider lurched forward. There was a popping sound, and Paddy the Pooka materialized in his disguise as a donkey.

"Stop the spider, Abby," gasped Paddy. "It mustn't be allowed to get to Jack and Josiah."

"I know," shouted Abby.

Baal had to pass her to catch up with Jack and Josiah. She jumped in front of Baal, took Jack Elvin's clasp knife from her pocket and stabbed the gigantic creature in one of his legs.

Baal squealed with rage and started to snap at her with his great jaws. She stabbed again.

Baal stopped, determined now to finish off Abby before going after Jack Elvin.

Dodging the vicious jaws of the giant spider, Abby called out, "Benbow!"

The great bird swooped down and plucked her away.

"Keep me close to Baal," she shouted, and Benbow hovered just out of reach of the Spider's hideous jaws.

"Baal!" screamed Wolfbane hysterically. "Kill the other two, quickly. I command you!"

But Jack Elvin and Josiah Bowsprit had already disappeared into the boundaries of Speller and were safe.

Sir Chadwick pressed forward, forcing Wolfbane to his knees.

"Isn't it time you took your carousel ride?" shouted Wolfbane as they heard the station clock chiming the hour.

"Hilda, Chaddy, get on my back, quick," shouted Paddy the Pooka. "You've got to get to the carousel."

"Come on, Abby," shouted Sir Chadwick and, breaking away from the fight, he swept Hilda away from Lucia and onto Paddy's back. Then he leaped up behind her.

"I'll catch up," shouted Abby, still dangling precariously from Benbow's legs, just close enough to tempt Baal.

Paddy wheeled away and began to gallop in the direction of Torgate with Hilda and Sir Chadwick clinging on and shouting for Abby and Benbow to follow them.

Still hovering just out of reach to distract Baal, Abby and Benbow circled about the giant spider's snapping jaws. Suddenly, Abby heard the distant sound of a train whistle and knew exactly what she must do.

Instead of following Sir Chadwick and Hilda along the Torgate Road, she took quite another direction. Enraged, Baal turned and chased her along the railway line.

Wolfbane, frothing with fury, thrust his mother back into the spectral carriage. As he leaped in behind her, he screamed, "After them!"

The carriage set off in pursuit of Sir Chadwick and Hilda. Baal continued to scuttle after Benbow and Abby.

"Into the railway tunnel, Benbow," shouted Abby. "But make sure you stay *very close* to the roof."

Benbow reached the tunnel entrance only just ahead of Baal's snapping jaws. They plunged into its darkness. Up ahead, Abby could hear the thunderous roar of the London train rushing toward them.

Moments later, she felt the heat from the train's smoke-stack engulf her body as it thundered beneath them. Benbow was thrown from side to side in the turbulence. But it was too late for Baal. Abby heard a massive thudding squelch. She sighed with relief, knowing what grim fate had finally befallen the giant spider.

When they emerged into daylight once more, Benbow flew high above Darkwood Forest. Abby looked down and saw Paddy galloping toward Torgate with Wolfbane chasing behind in the spectral carriage.

"Faster, Benbow," she shouted, and the bird surged forward. They passed above the carriage and caught up with Sir Chadwick and Hilda just after Paddy had come to a clattering halt next to the fair.

"Quick, all aboard the carousel," shouted Sir Chadwick to Abby and Hilda.

"What about Benbow and Paddy?" Abby gasped breathlessly.

"Don't worry about us, darlin', we'll make our own arrangements," said Paddy quickly. "See you soon."

Sir Chadwick handed the tickets to the attendant, a tall, thin man with a walrus mustache, and the carousel began to turn just as Wolfbane's carriage thundered into sight.

38

The Ride Home

As the carousel began to spin faster and faster, Abby clung on with all her might. To her horror, she realized that the spectral carriage was galloping alongside them as the carousel whirled through time.

The coachman urged the skeletal horses closer and closer. Wolfbane and his mother were leaning out to grab Abby with their clawlike hands. She turned her head and saw Sir Chadwick take the lamp from his pocket.

"Duck down, Abby," he shouted and threw the device into the spectral carriage.

The horses reared, and there was a shattering explosion. The carriage vanished in a thick black cloud of dust. As it cleared, Abby saw that the blast had knocked Sir Chadwick and Hilda off the carousel.

"Oh, no!" she cried.

Helpless, and clinging on for dear life, she watched as they tumbled farther and farther away into the dark infinity of space.

The carousel whirled on. The tears Abby shed for her friends were blown from her cheeks and away into space and time.

Gradually, the carousel came to a stop. Abby sat with her head bowed. When she finally opened her eyes, she shook her head in bewilderment. Was she still in the past?

The Torgate to which she had returned was quite different from the one she had first known. Instead of being just a set of blackened stumps, the pier stood in all its original gaudy splendor. There was no sign of the sharp pebbles and rocks that had marred the beach. It was covered with golden sand.

Abby looked along the promenade, which was swept clean. The thunderous loudspeakers that had blared out electronic music were gone. A tuneful pipe organ played cheerful music in the fair. All the rides and sideshows were brightly painted and glowed with rows of lights.

There was no smell of Sid Rollin's hamburgers. The sea air was crisp and fresh with a slight tang of fish and chips and cotton candy.

Instead of the concrete and neon streetlights, the original gas lamps still stood, festooned with flower baskets. In fact, flowers bloomed everywhere. To her further astonishment, standing in a place of honor next to the floral clock was the *Torgate Belle*, as bright and shiny as when Abby had last seen her.

The town looked delightful in the summer sunshine and the tourists were all obviously very happy.

There was no sign of Sir Chadwick and Hilda. But Abby's heart leaped as she saw two familiar figures.

Paddy the Pooka, in human form, stood at the entrance to the pier. Benbow was perched on the rails beside him. She crossed the promenade and ran to greet them.

"Welcome back, me darlin' girl," said Paddy.

"Paddy, Benbow," she cried. "Sir Chadwick and Hilda are lost in time."

"Oh, I think they're going to be all right," said Paddy soothingly. "Now, you hop aboard Benbow. You've got a wedding to go to."

Abby looked down and was astonished to see she was wearing her bridesmaid's dress. Suddenly hopeful, she called out, "Home, Benbow," and seized the great bird's feet.

Up and up they flew, out of Torgate, over Darkwood Manor and across the forest until she could see the familiar cliffs of Speller and the lighthouse beneath her. The Time Freeze had been lifted.

She could hear the Speller Town Band playing and, as Benbow swooped down onto the path from the lighthouse, she saw Hilda and the wedding party just setting out.

Benbow landed her beside Spike, who was looking splendid in his uniform.

He glanced at her and asked, "Where have you been, Abby? Sir Chadwick and Hilda arrived on Paddy's back an hour ago."

"I'll tell you later," said Abby, grinning as the wedding procession began its descent down the cobbled path to the church where Sir Chadwick was waiting.

On the cliffs above Speller, two tall figures dressed in black coats and striped trousers looked down on the church where the wedding was taking place. They were the Permanent Undersecretaries from the Ministry of Time and the Ministry of Coincidence, and they both held bulging files under their arms.

"I think we managed the whole business rather well," said the Wizard of Time with deep satisfaction.

"We did alter the present a little," replied the Wizard of Coincidence.

The Wizard of Time shrugged. "Nothing serious, and look what was gained. Torgate is once more a delightful seaside town."

"And Hilda Bluebell, or should I say Lady Street, now knows who she really is," said his companion.

"Wolfbane and his mother are lost in time."

"And Abby Clover gained some valuable experience. She really is very promising."

"We couldn't have done it without Paddy the Pooka."

"Yes, he really is one of our very best agents."

"So, the Torgate business is finally closed," said the Wizard of Time.

"I think so," said the Wizard of Coincidence and, with satisfied laughter, they both threw their bulging files into the air.

A light wind caught the fluttering papers and slowly shredded them into a cloud of confetti, which was borne on the breeze to fall on Hilda and Sir Chadwick as they left the church to the sound of the Speller Town Band playing "Sunshine Millionaire."

About the Author
by Wolfbane

When Michael Molloy was a small boy I had high hopes for him. He was noisy at home, inattentive at school, and constantly disrespectful toward his elders and betters.

Unfortunately, his manner changed somewhat when he attended art school. And when he got a job as a copy boy on a newspaper my disappointment found new bounds. He actually began to enjoy his work! So much so, he eventually became the editor.

He and his wife, Sandy, live in Ealing, near London. They have three daughters, Jane, Kate, and Alex, and a granddaughter named Georgia. She is the reason he began writing children's books.

Oh, he also has two dogs called Fred and Daisy. Personally, I hate them all! (Actually, they might taste rather good in my mother's carrion stew.)

Not too long ago, Abby Clover knew
nothing of witches or magic.
Then she met a mysterious stranger
and her life changed forever.
Find out how it all began in The Witch Trade.

Just before Abby slipped her hands from the straps she spoke to Benbow. "Keep circling the building. If I need you in a hurry I'll shout out," she whispered. Benbow nodded and took off again.

Abby crouched down in sudden fear because she could see a few of the strange, apelike figures prowling around the tangled garbage. Then she remembered she was invisible and slowly stood up.

She whispered into her seashell to tell Starlight about the trolls nearby.

"Take care," he said. "They can be very dangerous."

"What exactly are trolls, Captain Starlight?" she asked softly.

"A very nasty type of creature that used to be found in the forests of central Europe," he answered. "We never had them in America. They used to steal children, so they say."

"What for?"

Starlight paused. "Well, the story said they liked to keep them as slaves until the children grew big enough to eat. Night Witches like trolls because they're stupid and wicked but easy to train. Best to keep clear of them, Abby."

"I'll keep as clear as I can," she replied, looking up. Benbow was visible now and still hovering above her. Two of the prowling trolls nearby stared at him, momentarily puzzled by his sudden appearance. Abby shuddered to see their snouty faces gazing into the sky, as if they were sniffing for food.

She quickly found the entrance to the tunnel and reeled back for a moment, gasping at the dreadful smell. It was like a mixture of bad eggs, sewers, and old boiled cabbage water. Abby knew roughly where she was heading. When they had studied the inside of the building earlier she had noticed a room where the walls were covered with maps. It was off to one side of a much larger chamber that was filled with rows of empty benches.

Now, she hurried through the tunnel. It curved down through the building in a steep slope. She was glad to see there were signposts and notices. Occasionally, Night Witches swooped above her and she had to keep ducking her head.

Suddenly, ahead, she saw a flurry of witches gathering to enter a room. The sign above the door said COURT NUMBER ONE in bold letters and below, in smaller type, *Leading to Trophy Room* — exactly what she'd been seeking.

Although the witches disgusted her, Abby joined the throng to squeeze inside the chamber. She slipped into a space behind the door. Night Witches were taking the seats on the banks of benches that lined each side of the room. Abby could now see that it was furnished as a courtroom with a dock for a prisoner and a raised bench for a judge.

Like the rest of the building, the room smelled awful and the Night Witches were all scratching themselves as they jabbered together in subdued voices. Most of them had ragged yellowish teeth and Abby noticed that even the younger ones often showed black gaps where teeth should be.

Now, Abby could study them in detail. They were an ugly

bunch, some fat and some thin, and all ages. But, apart from the black cloaks they wore, the only thing they had in common was how grubby they were. She had never seen so much greasy hair and so many dirty fingernails and ingrained dirt.

The older men wore stained suits and the younger ones dirty casual clothes. The women all seemed to favor shabby, dull-colored dresses that trailed along the floor. Judging from their fish-white complexions they obviously didn't spend much time in daylight.

When the court was full, a witch who was standing at a table below the judge's bench banged on the table with a gavel and said, "Silence. All rise for her supreme eminence, Judge Stakeheart."

The Night Witches rose to their feet and a very old woman with straggly hair and a face covered in warts entered. She was wearing a cloak, tattered and green with age. It flapped around her as she shuffled toward the high seat behind the bench.

"Be seated," the clerk commanded. "Bring in the prisoner."

A door opened at the back of the court and two trolls entered escorting a young woman who hung her head so that long greasy hair obscured her face. She was enveloped in a grubby Night Witch's cloak.

"Remove her cloak," the judge ordered.

One of the trolls wrenched it off to reveal that the prisoner was wearing a clean pale-yellow dress. The other troll snatched the greasy wig from her head, and shining red hair tumbled around her shoulders.

There was a collective gasp of surprise from the court. The young woman threw back her head and gazed around the court defiantly.

"What are the charges?" Judge Stakeheart asked.

An extremely fat Night Witch, who had been lolling at one of the tables in front of the bench and scratching the stains on his vest, rose to his feet and said, "If it please Your Eminence, this creature known to us, until she was apprehended, as Gretchen Cringe, is in fact a Light Witch! She joined our order under false pretences to gain access to our secrets."

"What evidence do you have?"

"The evidence of your own eyes, Your Eminence. As you observe, beneath her cloak she wears clean clothes. When she was examined, there were no lice or fleas about her person, and . . ." The accuser hesitated.

"It is so horrible, Your Eminence, I did not want to offend your sensibilities."

"Thank you for your delicacy, but pray continue."

"She smells of flowers."

This revelation caused a moan of horror to ripple through the court.

"How was she apprehended?" the judge asked when the court was silent.

"She was trying to release a polar bear that was the subject of experiments in the research department."

"Enough," the judge commanded. She addressed the accused.

"Do you have anything to say before I pass sentence?"

The girl in the dock looked around the room with contempt. "Only that I am Sally Oak of the Ancient Order of Light Witches. I am immune to your punishments, as you well know. I demand to be released immediately."

The judge gave a sharp laugh. "You are quite wrong, young woman. It was once the case that Light Witches were immune to our spells, but our strength has increased mightily since then. We have devised a machine, powered by Black Dust, that will soon be used on all your brethren. Therefore, I sentence you to be atomized and spend all eternity in the prison we have devised for Light Witches."

The court started to applaud, but Judge Stakeheart held up a clawlike hand. "Bring in the prototype of the Atomizer."

A door opened and a group of trolls pushed in a machine that looked to Abby like a huge flashlight mounted on wheels. Thick cables spewed from the end.

"So you can fully appreciate the severity of your punishment, Sally Oak," the judge continued, "we shall demonstrate the Atomizer on the polar bear you tried to release. Bring it in."

More trolls entered with a great white bear that was secured with chains. The trolls were armed with batons that gave electric shocks to the creature. They positioned it before the Atomizer.

"Begin," the judge ordered and one of the trolls pulled a lever at the side of the machine. There was a sound like the distant crying of a lost child and to Abby's horror a clear rectangle formed around the bear and began to shrink until it was smaller than a matchbox. The Night Witches sent up shrieks of approval.

"Hand it to the prisoner," Judge Stakeheart ordered.

Sally Oak took the tiny object from the troll and held it tenderly. "Poor bear," she said and tears trickled down her cheeks. When she looked up, her eyes were blazing defiantly. "A curse on you Night Witches for your vile cruelties. What has this poor creature done to you that you should torture it so?"

"Save your pity for yourself," the judge answered and turned to the trolls. "Carry out the sentence."